# NOTTZ '08

## A novel

JOE CASSIUS

THE CHOIR PRESS

First published in the United Kingdom in 2025 by
The Choir Press

ISBN 978-1-78963-539-3

Joe Cassius is also a psychotherapist.
He lives and works alone.
His previous works are *All is Wild, All is Silent* and
*This Weirdish Wild Space.*

for

the beautifully mad

to those who didn't quite make it back

# Contents

Day One

# The Date

'Tied up in Nottz, with a Z, you cunt.'

Sleaford Mods

# Pulled Pork

*Raasclaat. Ragamuffin. Ramshackle. Rigmarole.*

Am meeting some girl called Collette tonight although I can't remember what she looks like. My mate Neal said she was *a bit on the big side*. Big but not too big.

Big-*ish*. Blonde. Busty.

Chunky, cheerful.

*I'd do her,* he said.

When I met her that day, I was not drunk. But then I wasn't sober, either. It was early afternoon and I was up and out of the hangover. Pint no. 2, down, done.

The slow clanking chains of my inner machinery, rollercoaster back on the rise.

I was in that adrift state, that in-between state.

That floaty, fuddled, fearless place where nothing was impossible.

Just went up to her and said the first thing that popped into my head and popped out of my mouth. Plopped into her ear and stopped her in her tracks.

*Dontcha know … I'm your little red rooster.*

*What?*

Confused, amused. Only for her face to light up with a broad beaming smile.

*That smile of yours … almost makes me wish I was a lesbian.*

*You're fuckin' nuts!*

Giant, lovable laughter; bare shoulders and big tits, bouncing.

Her digits found their way into my phone and off she went with her mates, a wicked smile disappearing out the door.

Now she's just a blonde blur in my mind, a gold glimmer of a girl.

The only good thing I remember, from my last five-day bender.

# Metamorphosis

I tried to jump off at day 3, but it didn't work out. I came close, though. Even had the props in place. Preparations made. Door locked. Phone off. Curtains closed. Two glasses by my bed. One to drink water from and the other to piss in. A bowl of fruit. A stack of porn. CDs: Fleetwood Mac. Dylan. Cohen. Bruce. Tom Petty and Enya. Holst's *Planets* for cosmic travel. Madonna's *Immaculate Collection* for when I really wanted to fuck myself up. Oasis' early stuff, Chili Peppers' later stuff.

Yep. The day of DTs was set. I was ready. Ready for my rattle.

The Rattle Day.

Twenty-four hours of pure clean evil. A shining hell.

Here in my second-storey bedsit overlooking Gedling shops. This simple box-like room, tilted and slowly revolving on its axis. Scarlett Johansson on one wall. Van Gogh's *Noon: Rest from Work* on the other. Tiny telly at the foot of the bed. Buddha lying across my windowsill and a pair of baby-blue dumbbells wedged in the corner.

Let the convalescence commence.

I curled up under the bed sheets like Kafka's insect. Twitchy, sweaty and scared to death. Eyes slowing and ready to fall, landing on one object and then another.

Something was bothering me, springing my eyelids open every few seconds. A letter lying on the floor, partially obscured by the remote control. It had been ripped open sometime mid-bender. I don't remember it. I don't remember opening it, and I definitely don't remember reading it. Through the shards of paper and the screwed-to-a-ball envelope I saw red writing and knew it wasn't good. My heart already starting to twist in my chest, stomach folding in on itself. My skull filling with dread. I reached out, pinching at the corner, sliding it towards me.

Letter heading: NOTTINGHAM JUSTICE CENTRE

*Oh. Fuck.*

In bold black accusatory font:

TO ATTEND AT 2PM

Those words screamed right at me.

Next place for my eyes was the digital clock on the other side of the room: 12:07.

*Fucking. Hell.*

4

I couldn't move. I couldn't move but I had to move. I couldn't move. Not one bit. Not an inch. This body straitjacketed and saturated with stagnant alcohol sweats. Temperature at both sides of the spectrum, like influenza. Something cruel was crawling right through my insides. Burrowing into my brain, setting my emotions alight. Horrible, fugitive emotions. In bits.

I was ... absolutely terrified.

And I was supposed to take all this and head on to the outside world.

And I was supposed to take this package of self-abuse and self-loathing and attend the magistrates' court, the NOTTINGHAM JUSTICE CENTRE, in less than two hours?

I skim-read more of the letter and its none-too-subtle threats ... *failure to surrender ... will take immediate effect ... custodial sentence.*

### Scarlett Johansson

Rolling back over, considering my options, staring at the wall and trying to find an answer there. Miss S Johansson's once heavenly face of infinite kindness now had something else in there. *Hmm.* The beauty spot on her right cheek now lasered into the depths of my soul. Her endless eyes and signature lips openly mocking me:

*Just who the fuck are you?*

*I don't know, Scarlett.*
*Just. Who. The. Fuck. Are. Ya?*
*I. Just. Don't. Fucking. Know.*
*I mean, what kind of man are you, boy?*
*I don't know.*
*You wanna go back to prison or what?*
*Nah.*
*Then you better get moving. You better get UP.*

I moved and my back broke. Groaning first, then a whimper. One foot on the floor and then the second foot on the floor. She's right; I have to do this. I have to move. I have to put on clothes and leave this flat and go outside. I have to get on the bus and go back into town and go to court.

But how?
  But really, how?

I looked at the empty bottles by the bin and saw it as a sign, a message from the gods.

Just a few to top me up and tip me off, put me on a level and break me even. Save my soul. There was a certain performance I had to pull off, and I needed to be on form to convince *them* that I was just a good person caught in a bad situation.

Going in like this was a mistake. Going in like this was suicide.
  Therefore, having another day on it was responsible behaviour.
  This was to be day no. 4.

Crossing the road to the off-licence scared me to death. The four-inch kerb had a 100ft drop the other side. My toes curled over the edge and I held my breath. The cars were too fast, and someone was going to smash me in the face for something I had done in the past. Outside simply wasn't safe.

Inside, and I had to put the coins on the counter.
  *All right, Robin?*
  He looked at my tremulous hands, so I buried them into the kangaroo pouch of my hoodie.
  *Getting warmer out there, yeah? April and all that.*
  Kept my head down the whole time. Made some kind of noise to answer him.
  His smile was sly and superior.
  *Someone was askin' after you. Askin' if you still lived over the road.*
  Oh.
  *Yeah, but I told 'em nuffink.*
  Yeah.
  *Not my business at the end of the day.*

I took my tins of medicine and got the fuck out of there. Nosy fuckin' Paki.

Every cunt out here plays head games.

On the bus and I tell myself ... tell myself to watch the booze. I'm already at the bottom of the first can. Just these two, I tell myself. Just these two tins and that's it.

That's enough. I want recovery from the withdrawal and no more. I really don't want a day no. 4. And I really don't want to be booked on a second charge for wobbling into court blindo. I crack the second can and already feel a damn sight better.

It has lifted. There is light.

I am lighter. I am lifted.

Something dark and troubling starts to melt away.

I almost feel cured. Already. I almost feel good. I almost feel

*excited.*

The kinda fit chavvy girl with a teenage arse makes a sniffing sound and switches seats. Away from me. She kisses her teeth and rolls her eyes and opens a window. And a father with a young son shows a similar displeasure. I hear him say to the curious boy in a low voice, *Don't stare.*

And maybe the bus driver too catches my eye in the rear-view, and maybe I don't care about none of this – just drink my drink and think my think and feel my feel and wonder where I will end up next.

## The Bridewell Bar

The name above the door was actually the *Bentinck Hotel*. But I called it Bridewell on account of it being opposite Bridewell Police Station. Down by the canal, next to the court, opposite the Waterfront. Whenever I was banged up in the holding cells, I was sure to be there the following morning, sipping a pint while putting my shoelaces back in. Body sore from a night on that thin rectangle of blue plastic. Graffiti tattooed on my brain from the last eight hours.

*FUCK FILTH*
*SHOTTINGHAM 08*
*MEDDERS MAN IS PUSSY OLE ... SV 4 EVER!*
*NFFC*
*PC BROWN FUCKS HIS MOTHER WITH A TRUNSHON*
*TONY 4 SARAH*
*ONLY GOD CAN JUDGE ME*
*BILBOROUGH MO DANGER CREW*
*NG 2*
*MUFC*
*RADDY MAN IS BATTY MAN*
*WASTE OF TIME, LIFE ON HOLD*
*CHERL COLE IS FIT*
*MANZ WILL GET 45, STEP TO ME SOLO*
*PIGZ*
*PRISON IZ A PLAYGROWND*
*LOVE SHEREECE 4EVER*
*WHY ALL WAYS ME?*
*FUCK FEDZ*

Bridewell was bang next to the train station. Its bar V-shaped and wooden, saloon-style. Frosted windows picked at into messy spy holes so you could look out onto the street. Nicotine-stained walls as the interior designer obviously hasn't visited since the ban. Lamp lights and wallpaper straight from a 1970s living room. Its clientele varied; from lonely drunks to customers from the hotel above. Revved-up football firms fresh from the station to people of the court, victims going in, criminals coming out, maybe the odd cheap solicitor making notes before a case. It had that waiting room quality. Everyone belonged; no one belonged. It did the trick for me that afternoon. Two pints sunk in quick succession and the paranoia was squashed, leaving a glow of confidence and purpose. Headed down the cobbled walkway to the huge glass palace of the magistrates' court. Through the metal detectors and up to court No. 2. Booked in, waited. Watched scrawny youths in oversized suits limping across the floor, big white trainers, thick gold chains; lips pursed defiantly beneath a bum-fluff tash. I had a quick briefing with my solicitor, which seemed pointless as I was pleading guilty. Then on to the usher, tiny black glasses on the tip of her tiny pink nose.

Her voice all posh-sexy and aloof as she asked my name.

*Robin Goode.*

There was always a curious reaction to my name.

Finally, I was in the firing line of the magistrates. My head down obediently. The authoritative silence, a polite cough and the rustling of papers. My apologetic speech, which was executed like an assassin, before being given a meagre £175 fine.

No sentence. No community service.

I left the court, a triumph.

The thing that had saved me was the thing that had put me there in the first place:

*alcohol.*

I was lucky. I took this as a sign to change, change my ways.

Start over. Start fresh. Start something new.

To do this, I had to take out the one thing that was at the core of everything:

*alcohol.*

Back in the Bridewell, arse plonked on those scarred seats. Their guts spewed up in bubbling rivulets of sponge. I had a toast with the old boy next to me.

*To a hundred-and-seventy-five-pound fine!*

We clinked glasses before joining the tail end of Monday Club.

Thurland followed by Flairs followed by Bar Schnapps.

This was day no. 4.

There will be no day no. 5.

Tomorrow, I will withdraw and rattle.

No court. No work. No appointments. No nothing.

Nothing but the rattle.

*Rattle, rattle, rattle.*

# Lucy Kite

The mirror is better than it was three days ago. I'm a man again. A twenty-seven-year-old boy who has been around a lifetime. I'm a blue-eyed, pale-faced Charlie of Irish descent. I'm sort of tall but not so much so. Sort of good-looking but not really. I'm stick-thin and as hairless as a dolphin. My hair is black and thick and wavy and impossible. I look different at different times, depending on which phase of the bender I'm at. I start as David Tennant and end as Richard Ashcroft.

It's all a question of taste.

People say I have *charisma*, whatever that means.

Overall, I don't believe them.

Mostly, I'm just normal-looking.

Your Average Joe, in every sense of the word.

My flat is back to some kind of order. Bed made. Bottles banked. I've cleaned out the mould from the fridge, and Scarlett's face is kind again. I always say that the state of my living space represents the state of my mind. I can only take so much quiet, though, so the TV goes on in the background as I pace and fix and faff and waste time ...

*Regional news now ... Derby, Leicester, Nottingham ... Brothers Colin and Dave Gunn ... Crime lords of the Bestwood Estate ... Bestwood Cartel ... are set to appeal ... a stabbing in Broxtowe ... a shooting in St Ann's ... and now for brighter news ... West Bridgford ... last year's winners of the national Flowers in Bloom Award are set to defend their title ... now here's the sport with Mike ... Football ... Forest shit, Notts County even shitter ... boxing ... Carl 'The Cobra' Froch fights back on home soil next month at the Trent FM Nottingham Arena as he takes on the formidable super middleweight ... Polish Albert Rybacki ... and now for the weather with Lucy Kite ...*

Lucy Kite. Her name grabs me like it always does. My balls skip a beat and my heart tingles. My little weather girl. Sunny, smiley and compact, bent back, with her chocolate hair cascading down the screen, her hands sweeping rain away as bulbs of sun burst at the edges of her fingertips ... I look back at the too-much beauty of Scarlett Johansson and decide that Lucy is a better fit, a better match, more real, much closer to what I'm looking for, more ...

*accessible* ... yep, on a good day ... at the right time and place and with just the right amount of alcohol in me, I could very well pull ...

Ring of my phone breaks the daydream.

I bend down to see a name flashing in the centre of the screen.


### Cassidy

She always starts the conversation by simply stating my name.

*Robin.*

*My biological sister.*

*You still sober or what?*

*Or what.*

*What?*

*I am.*

*What?*

*Still sober.*

*Fank fuck.*

*Thanks.*

*Still goin' on that date or what?*

*Far as I know.*

*What does that mean?*

*Means as far as I know, I'm still going.*

*She cancelled or somefink?*

*Nah, she hasn't cancelled.*

*Fucked it up, ain't yar?*

*Nah.*

*Bet you have.*

*No.*

*Bet you called her when you were pissed, dint yar?*

*I haven't been pissed.*

*How long you been sober then?*

*Well.*

*How many days?*

*Four, five.*

*So you goin' or what then?*

*On the date?*

*Yeah, ya goin'?*

*Yeah, I'm goin'.*

*Don't fuck it up.*
*Not planning to.*
*What's her name again?*
For a moment, I had to think.
*Collette.*
*She a chav or somefink?*
*Nah, I reckon she's quite posh actually.*
*Posh?*
*Well, not posh, just not—*
*Fort you said you don't remember her.*
*I don't remember her face, but I remember her voice.*
*That don't even make no goddamn sense.*
*I don't know.*
*Where you meet again?*
*Ye Olde Trip to Jerusalem, so I've been told.*
*I don't even know what that means.*
*You're FROM Nottingham.*
*Yeah, so?*
*And you don't know ... Cassidy, it's the oldest inn in—*
*Oh, shut up then, you know I don't go out or nuffink.*
*Cass, you really should—*
*Isn't she like fat or somefink?*
*Who?*
*Dis gal.*
*Oh. Yeah. Voluptuous, Neal said.*
*Yeah, well, he don't know nowt.*
*I better get ready, Cass. I don't wanna be—*
*You better not be late, Robin.*
*I won't.*
*Have you had a shave?*
*Fuck's sake, Cass.*
*Yeah, well, you look like a tramp uvverwise.*
*I've got stubble.*
*Get a shave, ya tramp.*
*Designer stubble, Cass.*
*Where you meeting again?*
*Saltwater.*
*Never heard of it.*
*I know.*
*Yeah, well, I hope it goes well, and you better let me know.*

*I will.*

*Let me know first fing, yeah?*

*I will.*

*Don't fuck it up, Robin, cah it's about time you seckled down.*

*You ain't settled down.*

*That's different.*

*I'm going.*

*You're not gettin' any younger, ya know.*

*I know.*

*She sounds good for you.*

*What? You don't even know her.*

*Yeah, well, she's fat, innit.*

*Fuck's that gotta do with owt?*

*Skinny bitches are too uptight.*

*You're a skinny bitch.*

*Yeah, and I'm uptight.*

*Yeah. Well. I better—*

*She sounds perfect for you.*

*I want Lucy Kite.*

*What?*

*Nothing.*

*And don't start being weird, cah you'll scare her off.*

*I won't.*

*And don't mention prison.*

*I won't.*

*Don't be too full-on.*

*I won't.*

*Don't be too confident, cah girls don't like that, not really.*

*I won't.*

*Have a shave and don't be late.*

*I will and I won't.*

*What?*

*I hear what you're saying.*

*And ... Robin.*

*What?*

*More than anything, more than all the above ...*

*Yeah?*

*Don't get drunk.*

The line dies. Cassidy is gone.

## 'Tom Hark' (Originally Performed by The Piranhas).

I drink a pint of full-fat milk. Lucy Kite is gone and *Hollyoaks* replaces her. Soaps are bad at the best of times but *this*. At first, I thought it was a spoof. A piss-take. This acting and these storylines. No wonder people are fucked, filling their brains with this garbage. Tawdry entertainment for teenagers and thick cunts. My sister Cassidy loves this shit. She calls me an arrogant prick who thinks I'm better than everyone although I don't know what she means. I close down the TV and stick on some tunes. A song I always listen to as I head out the door. Kind of a tradition thing although I don't know why or where this came from. Probably something to do with staying on the sunny side of the mind, a reminder that life isn't as serious as we think. I bop about as I make the final touches to my unpredictable appearance. The song lyrics giddy in my mouth.

*Does anybody know how long to World War 3? I wanna know, I wanna book me holiday ... the whole thing's daft ... I don't know why ... you have to laugh ... or else you cry ... you have to live ... or else you die ...*

I take my keys and wallet and phone. Scarlett is looking right at me as I close the door. Today, her expression is neutral. Like she is undecided about me.

## Hard Rock Cafe

Dusk and warmth, the bus moves through it. Almost that tropical feeling of being abroad. Neon ripples the window, my dark reflection collapsing and reforming. I marvel at Mapperley Top. How much this has changed in the last six months. Before, it was just a little strip of dusty charity shops and spit 'n' sawdust pubs. Now it's a thriving mini-city, pulsing with takeaways, restaurants and a giant Wetherspoons. Seeing the people move about in the lighted windows makes my stomach bite down with a need of something. I lick my lips and try to put my mind elsewhere as the green double-decker hurtles down Woodborough Road, towards the lights of the city.

I'm in town just before seven. Half an hour early, half an hour to waste. Standing in the horseshoe-shaped road of King Street/Queen Street. Right on the spot where the Brian Clough statue is set to be unveiled in November. The buildings are beautiful here, intricate Edwardian architecture that bends over and kisses the street.

Fuck's sake. Hark at me.

I sometimes catch myself thinking in sentences like this and wonder.

*Intricate Edwardian architecture that bends over and kisses the street.*

Across the far side of the market square is another Wetherspoons.

Even from here I can hear *that* noise.

That squabble. That hassle 'n' hustle. A dirty murmur.

There's a blur of figures moving around outside, smoking, pacing, about to kick off.

It looks like summer. It looks like Christmas.

This time last week, I was in there, amongst it. Steaming. Sloshed. Smashed.

Wrecked and blindo. Mouthing off. Being a cunt.

Now I'm on a date. Meeting a girl in a fancy wine bar. Smart and sound and sober. Doing something nice, something pleasant. Civilised, one may say. Looking up. Looking up at the *intricate Edwardian architecture that bends over and kisses the street.*

The council house bell gongs seven times. Half an hour early, half an hour to waste.

I turn a 180 and neon smacks me in the face, eyes locked with the universally recognised sign of the Hard Rock Cafe.

Half an hour?

I could hit this, grab an orange. Sit. Relax. Get in the mood.

Half an hour?

No point wandering the streets.

There's a bar before me and a cute girl behind it.

A sweet smile and a courteous nod of the head. Hand wrapped around the pump, ready to serve.

I open my mouth. *San Miguel.*

I am shocked by these words and I don't know where they've come from.

San. Miguel.

I want to take them back, only it's too late. She begins filling me up.

Pint poised, cocked. Nozzle pressed. A slow thin arc, webbing the glass.

By the time it is poured, I have given up, given in, accepted this with a heavy sigh of surrender.

It's a pint, so what?

It's a simple pint to loosen up and kill time. It's the most normal/natural thing in the world, so why am I vexing? Why am I thinking this way? Why this unnecessary pressure on myself?

Cute Bargirl studies me as I draw out my wallet. Dimples, small knowing eyes.

It's like she's closely watching these thoughts as I turn them over. *Is this the thought process of an addict? Is this how they think? Is this what I am, an al—? Nah, I'm not, can't be. Been sober for five days straight and haven't felt the urge for a single drop.*

With this deductive reasoning, I exhale and relax.

Cute Bargirl nodding away as she takes my dollar, agreeing with me, half letting me off. *If you say so, Mister.*

San Miguel and I take a seat. He sits solidly before me, bubbling away. His beauty is undeniable. I watch him and he watches me. My reflection widening as I rotate the glass, stretching clownishly like those mirrors at Goose Fair. His beauty is unmatched. I pick him up and tilt him towards me. Lip on rim, lapping it up. The liquid bouncing against my tongue, not taking him in yet. Taste buds burning and bursting as the senses fire up like a racing car.

*I know you. I know you. I've been here before.*

At last, a fully formed swallow, a whole gulp. A river rushes through me.

So crisp and so cold.

I drink, therefore I am. I drink I am drinking I am a drinker.

I watch myself from afar. Sat here under a framed Keith Richards shirt.

I drink. I drink San Miguel. A quarter of the way down him and there's a vibration in my groin.

Text:

*Hey, my little red rooster. Lol.*
*Sorry running a li'l L8. Maybe 15. That alright? X*

I reply:

*No, it's not alright.*
*An hour's detention.*
*My office  x*

Barely back in my pocket, vibrate.

*Spanked? X*

A twist in my guts and a stiffening in my pants.
    Alarmed and appalled and exhilarated by her accelerated sexual forwardness.

*Same again?*
With two fingers, my empty is pushed back towards Cute Bargirl.
*Hit me.*
She nods, clearly reading the word on my forehead: *Twat*.
Only an American or a twat or a twat pretending to be an American would use the line *Hit me*. Under this flirty frivolity, something more worrying is taking shape. I am now on my second pint. Second pint before going on a date, a first date.
*Oh, so what? She's late.*
*She's late, so what else am I supposed to do?*

Again, that sentence in my head: *It's the most normal/natural thing in the world.*

I take this one in with more ease and less guilt. Heart lit. Thoughts slowing with the turning of a tap. A certain glorious numbing of the brain. The sofa chair moulding my limbs like liquid. I turn and note the detail and definition of the Keith Richards shirt behind me, the dash of colour, the legend of it all. My arm keeps moving and my mouth keeps moving. My throat warm, my emotions calm.

*Tipsy is the welcome mat on the porch to the House of Chaos. Wipe your feet and step inside.*

Vibrate:

*Really, really, really*
*sorry hun but this damn tram is taking the piss!*
*Gonna b another 15.*
*Oh well, just means another spank :) x*

*Same again?*
My eyes shoot from glass to pump, *San Miguel.*
The red swirling letters of *S* and *M* beckoning me, teasing me, taunting me.
Almost a dare, almost a challenge.
Three pints, big deal.
I'm used to fifteen or more.
Three is nothing; three is foreplay.
A drop in the ocean.
Cute Bargirl is staring at me, waiting for an answer.
*Do it, do it.*
She looks at my forehead again, *Twat* rubbed off, replaced with *Prick.*

*Collette, I forgot to text her back.*
*Or did I?*
*Or do I need to?*

I reread the text and decide to let it hang, suspended in mystery.
I stay stood this time, working the pint in swift swallows, watching the agility of Cute Bargirl as she moves deftly around her working space.
*Working here long?*
Her eyes meet mine and in that moment I switch adjectives, *cute* for *beautiful.*
She does the same, *prick* for *cunt.*
*Long enough*, she says with a sigh.
I contemplate this sigh and what it could mean – the job or my predictable line of questioning?
*Like it?*

*Love it,* she says in full, unhidden sarcasm.

Vibrate:

*Here! x*

I ignore it and keep my attention on Beautiful Bargirl.
*Oh, come on, it can't be that bad, having the pleasure of slimy scumbags like me chatting you up every night. What's not to love?*
For some reason, this line lightens the load, takes out the sting and finds a way in.
*Oh, so that's what you've been doing, chatting me up?* she smiles. *I would never have known.*
I hold up my hands as if a gun was pointed at me.
*Same again?*
Miraculously, there is another empty in my hand. I try to work out what this new expression on her face means – amused, disgusted, impressed?
*Sure.*
*Boy, you can knock 'em back.*

Vibrate:

*Didn't your mother teach you that it's rude to keep a girl waiting?*

I note the immediate change in tone. Gone are the flirty abbreviations. Just the stark seriousness of a full sentence. Gone too is the kiss at the end.
My first instinct is to reply with, *This from the bitch who was late in the first place.*
My second instinct is to reply with, *My mother is dead.*
Instead, I go with, *On my way X.*
Erasing the kiss before pressing *Send.*
*Two can play that game, fattie.*

A mysterious little voice, far away, in the nether regions of my psyche, says:

*See, Robin, three little pints and already turning into a nasty cunt. This is what booze does. Haven't you learnt by now? This isn't YOU.*

I shake it off and stand tall.

*You ain't seen nothing yet,* I suddenly say to BB, a delayed answer to her previous comment.

*What?*

I take the fourth San Miguel and set him down, eyeing him with levelled aggression.

*Big night with the lads?* she says.

*Nah, first date with a girl.*

I don't look at her as I say that.

*But ...* I continue.

*Yeah?*

*If it doesn't work out between us, then ...*

That mysterious little voice again:

*Do this and My Mysterious Little Voice will no longer be able to keep you safe. I'll probably be extinguished, for the next four or five days.*

*You know how it works. You know the drill.*

*I am the last little bit of control you have left.*

I take San Miguel by the scruff of the neck.

*Don't.*

And down him in one, taking six or seven seconds.

I belch and wipe my mouth and slap down on the bar, hard.

Other people look over.

I point at BB and finish the rest of my sentence: *I'm coming back for you.*

Her eyes are wide and so is her mouth.

She looks at my forehead: *Twat, Prick, Cunt.*

By now, she has no more words.

# Saltwater

The council house bell gongs eight times as my feet hit the street. The dimensions of the outside world float before me as the night air sharpens around my face. The lights, swirly and smudged, suck in from the buildings.

I realise how late I am and how long I've kept her waiting.

Cross the zebra on Parliament Street, rounding the two pubs that stand back to back, Langtry's and The Turf Tavern, before walking into the five-storey entertainment palace of The Cornerhouse. Through the glass doors and up the escalator. A string of students coming down the other way. Hot little numbers clad as cavegirls, carrying clubs, more flesh than garment. One is pinched by her mate and lets out a scream, turning so fast that her long blonde hair slaps me across the mouth, a whiplash of honey.

*Sorry!*

I mock injury and stumble back and pull a funny face and do a little dance and bow before them. The nymph just cracks right up. Her picture-perfect pretty pout, wrinkling her nose, all the time holding eye contact as we move away from each other. I head up as she goes down.


The Cornerhouse has a hierarchical tier system of Dantesque proportions. The higher up you go, the better off you are. Revolution on ground floor, a funky Mex-bar midway and Saltwater on top. Underground is the hellish meat market of Jumpin' Jaks.

My benders often end up there.

Although now, tonight, I move in the opposite direction.

I move *up*.

Up to Saltwater, a starry, sparkly wine bar, penthouse-style. Footballers and WAGS. It-girls and business boys. Boxer Carl Froch and his entourage. The cast and crew of the latest Shane Meadows. Top-end cokeheads and property tycoons. Arran Bailey and his mob.

*Hope she's getting the first round in.*

She? I don't even know what she looks like, and as I approach the door, her name drops from my mind too. *Fuck.*

*Evening, boss.* Nice to have a bouncer that smiles and opens a door. Instead of the shitholes I normally frequent, where the greeting is an accusatory snarl and rough pat-down.

The place is packed, and I still haven't got a Scooby who I'm looking for. I was hoping that the booze on board might kick the memory back in.

I really don't remember what she looks like.

I scan the joint, hoping to see a smiley face or a raised hand. Jack shit and nothing.

To make it more head-fucky, there are several big blonde things knocking about, wandering the floor, taking a seat, stalking the bar. Just then, I see something head towards me and I draw breath. Stumpy legs, bingo wings and a face like Matt Lucas. I look at her and luckily she looks right through me, and walks on.

*Phew.*

Then the opposite; a voluptuous masterpiece with more curves than Brands Hatch. I try and catch eyes, only for a suited Adonis to step in and kiss her on the cheek.

*Damn.*

Vibrate:

*What's it like, knowing you're being watched?*

I look up and around.

Vibrate:

*Little boy lost.*

Part excited, part pissed off now.

Vibrate:

*I'll play with you no more.*
*Back wall, brown table.*
*Nice shirt btw x*

A modernised version of *Good Life* by Inner City carries me through the bar.

There she is.

Turning her knees, a hand through the hair, standing. Fuck, she's tall, and bigger than I remember, prettier too, much prettier, and I do feel that immediate thump in the gut. That magical *thing.*

*Whoa, you're taller than I remember*, she says, laughing.

*Funny, I was thinking the same thing.*

We hug and there's a frightening unfamiliarity to all this, and it's then I realise that I've not been on a date, *in years.*

Not since my mother—

*You all right then?* she says.

*I am. You?*

She nods awkwardly and I mirror that awkwardness by asking her the same thing twice. *All right?*

She nods fast and hard, hoping for this awkwardness to end, before quickly collaring a member of staff.

*Can we get some drinks over here?*

I'm impressed by this cos everyone else is crowded at the bar, and I wonder what kind of VIP shit she's packing. Even the dude seems confused, as if he's been tricked into something.

*Dry white wine, please*, she sings.

*Make that two*, I add.

*Is that a small or large?*

I check myself before giving the automatic, obvious response. Wait for the girl. Wait for Collette. Her lips do a funny thing while she contemplates comically, sparkle of mischief in her eye, before silently mouthing *Large,* the word filling her mouth like a yawn.

*Large it is*, I affirm, keeping the relief out of my voice.

She's beaming and cutely nervous, excited.

*Wine, wow! Now that is a first. Never been on a date with a guy that drinks wine.*

*I'm not a normal guy.*

*Evidently not.*

Suddenly my sister's sharp voice rings in my ear, from our conversation earlier:

*Don't be too confident.*

*Don't be too full-on.*

Awkwardness and nerves gone. She smiles and says more things, small talk of her journey into town. Characters on the tram and how young everyone looks and the girls who are wearing next to nothing and the posers who are in here.

*You called this joint, Miss*, I say.

*Yeah, I know*, she replies with a sigh. *Thought I'd try something different. Always wanted to check this place out.*

The wine arrives, two large globes full to the brim. *Wow.* Bar

Dude gives us the bill and my tabs nearly drop off. *I'll get these*, she says quickly. Thank fuck for that.

*I'll get the next round in. Wetherspoons, yeah?*

Her eyes flicker with amusement.

I watch her while she pays. Handbag, purse, bank card. Head to one side, hair running away from her. She talks through the music, from a big bright mouth with a dimple at each end. Lively, lovely cobalt eyes. She has a strange mix of being rooted but busy at the same time. Firmly planted in her chair but all the time fidgeting, fiddling, clocking everything around her. Her self-consciousness has something *fuck you* about it.

She puts me on edge; yet at the same time there's no place I'd rather be.

*So*, she says, *what do you do, and I don't necessarily mean work. I don't necessarily mean a job.*

Good cos I don't have one.

Well, I do, but it's barely a job. More of a half-job.

I'm on my final warning, and I really can't lose it or I'm proper in the shit.

I'm due in tomorrow.

The question gets harder when she reframes it like this:

*How do you spend your life?*

Fuck me. Ha. I note her confusion as she watches a momentary smile flash across my face. Thinking just exactly how I do ... spend my life.

Let me see. I turn this over in my head.

*Out. Out all the time and all the time out of it. Out skull, out bonce. Booze, pints. Shorts, shots. On the piss, on the wobble, on the snorkel. People. Strangers. Mates coming and going. Sniff, pills. Phet. Ket. Saturday night and Sunday morning. Monday Club – and Tuesday Club and Wednesday Club and Thursday Club and thank God it's Friday at last. People. Strangers. Jobs coming and going. Agency work. Agony work. Packing and picking in warehouses and whorehouses. Just enough. Just enough lolly and Pretty Polly so I can get back out, back downtown, back on the piss, back on the piss in this pissy shitty city. Counterfeit notes, counterfeit clothes. Goods off the clothes line, goods off the back of a van. Always a plan, always a scam. Teefin' and deceiving, fencing and forging, frauding. Conning. Getting caught and going court. Sorted, sold, bought. Paying fines and not paying fines.*

24

*Forgetting them and then getting new ones. Bigger ones. Community Service. Serving the community by wheeling grannies around Newark Market on a Saturday morning or calling out the bingo numbers or picking up litter in Bulwell or making keyrings for the spastics in Keyworth or Kegworth or wherever it was. People. Strangers. Enemies coming and going. Getting kicked in and dumped. Jumped from arseholes outside Thurland for gobbing off or copping off with the wrong gal. Someone else's Mrs, someone else's mam, someone else's ode duck. Shags with slags, down alleyways or up grass banks, behind the Robin Hood statue or up the castle walls. Getting clapped up and clapped off. Decked out. Down the GU or the Jobseekers on Monday morning, trying to sign something serious with my Parkinson hands, shaking all over the shop, tight-roping the dotted line. Can you walk in a straight one? says the copper and the fed ... filth ... aren't you fed up yet? Aren't you fed up with ALL this ... don't you want more out of life ... don't you want something better for ...*

*Yourself? Myself?*

She's staring right at me. And I don't realise she's staring until I look up at her sea-blues and say, *Golf.*

*What?*

*I like golf. Call me crazy but I like crazy golf.*

*We should play some sometime,* she says playfully. *You know they have it downstairs, right? Here at The Cornerhouse.*

*For our second date?*

*We'll see,* she says, a little childishly, hiding behind her wine glass.

We're slowly emptying them, halfway down already, and I almost forget the four pints already in there. In the system. Part of me panics but then I remember the old saying about the grape and grain. Wine then beer, queer. But beer then wine, fine.

I feel fine and she likes me, I can tell, but the above question did floor me a bit, and I'm aware that I've not answered it properly. Not answered it at all really. Mr Avoidant. I've run into a wall of shame, realising that this is the first time in a long time that I've had a conversation with someone outside of my degenerate bubble.

*How do you spend your life?*

A more apt and answerable question would have been, *How do you waste your life?*

25

Stuck for a moment, I predictably, and very uncreatively, turn the same question back at her.

*And what about you? What do you do and I don't necessarily mean work. How do you spend your life?*

She looks up to the chandeliers and seems to have a ready-made answer rolling around her head although a sudden attack of nerves appears to have jumbled her up.

*I, err, well, I'm just dead social really. I like to spend time with friends, and family. I like to drink. Oh, I just love to drink, and dance, occasionally. I also like to sing. People say I'm a really good singer, but I won't step foot near a karaoke unless I've had at LEAST one bottle of wine in me. I like to cook. Oh, I just love to cook. Indian food and Italian food. Mostly Thai and sometimes Chinese. Oh, and I love Mexican too. Just love it! Oh, and you can't beat a good Sunday roast. Although my mum always ends up taking over.*

Realising she's just lost herself, she brings herself back, and blushes, a bit.

*Err, what else? I play chess. I read. Look, I've got a confession. I'm a total geek! I read nerdy stuff like history and economics and all kinds of biographies about all kinds of boring people. And for work, well, I've got that very arduous occupation of being a student.*

*Studying?*

*Err, I'd rather not say.*

*Why?*

*You might judge me.*

*I won't.*

*Maybe later.*

*Maybe later what?*

*Maybe I'll tell you later.*

*You tell me when you feel like it, girl.*

At this, she pulls a certain kind of face and I can't quite read it. Good or bad, I just can't tell. It is then that I notice some quite bad scarring on the inside of her arms, partially hidden by a mass of bracelets on her wrists.

*Same again?* I say, slapping the table.

*Same again is good,* she says, vibrant and Americanized.

I collar Bar Dude. *Can we get some drinks over here?*

He swings around and leans in, *Sorry, but I'm afraid you're gonna hafta get your drinks at the bar this time,* before disappearing into the people, which have now doubled in size.

I look at Collette. My mouth hanging at the rejection. She smiles and puts her arms out.

*Hey,* she winks cockily, *you've either got it, or you don't.*

We take in two more large wines. The glorious lift of alcohol. Our conversation flows and our minds roll into each other and somehow my hand has found its way into hers. An invisible hour of giddy nothing. Everything I say is funny, and her laughter only makes me get *even* funnier.

*You're a fuckin' comedy god, you are!*

By now, she doesn't even try to hide the scars. Just sits, exposing her wrists, the soft white underbelly of her arm. With a slow thoughtless finger, I trace them.

*That feels nice.*

*Good.*

Silence. Looking at the people. Looking at each other. Drinking the wine.

*Quite surprised that day, actually.*

*What day?*

*Day we met. Day you rudely barged into my world.*

*Oh?*

*Asking me out the way you did.*

*What about it?*

*Guys don't ask me out like that.*

*Like what?*

*Singling me out.*

*What do you mean?*

*Well, they normally just fall into me, by happenstance.*

*Oh.*

*But you made a point of me.*

*Oh.*

*Guys don't normally ask me out like that. My friends, yeah, but not me.*

*What friends?*

*The friends I was with, didn't you see them?*

*Nope.*

*They're, like, fucking gorgeous, and then here's you, hitting on the fat girl. At first, I thought it was a wind-up.*

*What friends?*

*Oh. Fuck. Off!*

She looks emotional all of a sudden, and again I can't put my finger on what this means.

*Anyway,* she says, *where next?*

*C'mon,* I say, her hand still in mine. *Let's go.*

A modernised version of *Only Love Can Break Your Heart* by Saint Etienne carries us through the bar.

## Tantra

*Two large white wines.*

On the way there and I'm surprised by how drunk I feel. Well, not drunk, but *fuddled.* My words have their shoelaces untied, and they trip over each other occasionally. But this was a usual of mine; the relationship between brain, alcohol and mouth not finding its footing yet. If I can just push through two or three more drinks, at pace, then I will find that state I seek, that flawless flow of unstoppable eloquence and wit, those linguistic heights where only the few can tread. *Oh.* I also noticed that Collette broke hand-holding on the walk down here. This mystified me and gave me an uncharacteristic bout of doubt and anxiety. I look at her and try to put her in focus.

Tantra.

Around the edges are large playboy-style beds webbed in see-through drapes. Sexually symbolic pictures hang from the walls. A replica Brad Pitt uncorking a bottle of champagne between his legs. A woman standing behind a glass of red wine, cleverly representing the triangle of her bush. Collette has never been here before. She looks around, wide-eyed.

*Very sexy,* she says.

*Thanks. What about the bar?*

She shakes her head, and I'm not sure if this is a smile or a grimace.

*Bring all your women here?*

*Only the good ones.*

I have an awareness that my behaviour is becoming a little *cuntish.*

We take the drinks and head to the one vacant bed, cosily tucked away in the corner. I beat back the drapes and crash. The bed is blood-red, flecked with Barbie-pink. It has a dip in the middle and its shape resembles a giant tongue. In the centre there is a large wooden disc. We put the wines on it.

*I'm undecided about this place*, Collette says.

I start talking and more clumsiness spills from my mouth. Words slippery as eels, hard to catch, impossible to control.

*Are you drunk?*

A piece of pink strobe light lands on her face while she says that.

*Nah.*

*You so are.*

She looks at me pathetically.

I feel mad now. The only thing I am good at in life is drinking, and I'll be damned if I'm going to be mocked by some—

*I can see it in your eyes*, she confirms.

*Listen, babe,* I begin. *I had five pints before I met you.*

*What?*

Was it five, or four?

*I drank a fair bit before meeting you.*

*Yeah, you and me both*, she says.

I'm confused by this and don't know what she means.

She hangs back, smug, a rolling of the eyes followed by a fake yawn followed by the smallest of sly smiles. There seems to be some growing delight in the sense she is outdrinking her male date.

*I must be a lightweight*, I say.

*Must be.*

*Either that or you're a heavyweight.*

The comment goes down like a lead balloon, but somehow I manage to make it worse.

*I meant with the drink.*

*I know what you meant*, she snaps.

Like trying to cover a bad smell with a worse smell. I cringe for a moment and then counteract by doing what I do best:

The bar.

This time, I hit top shelf.

*Two double JDs and Coke.*

*I don't drink that*, says Collette on my return.

*More for me then*, I sing, swirling the ice clockwise around the glass.

*Why didn't you ask what I wanted?*

29

*I found a gap in the queue on my return from the toilet. I took my chance.*

*Okay.*

*I'll go back.*

*It's okay.*

*Really, I'll go back.*

*Can we just go to the next bar?*

I lean in suddenly and kiss her slow on the lips. I seem more surprised at this move than she does. She doesn't pull away, but she doesn't fall in love, either.


## At the Next Bar

At the next bar, Collette returns from the ladies' looking upset.

*Great, now what have I said?*

By now, I'm on fire and welcome all obstacles. My brain feels like Oscar Wilde, my body like Mike Tyson. I could talk the world down and walk through walls.

*What's eating you, my dear?*

Its wine again that sits before me.

*Nothing.*

*Tell it.*

There's a collected tear in her eye and red in her face. She looks down at her shoe.

*Just some pricks at the bar, taking the piss out of me.*

I look up to see two weasel-faced lads, glancing over, laughing.

*What they say?*

*Nothing important enough to remember.*

*But important enough to hurt you.*

*Can we just forget it?*

Before I know it, I'm on my feet, taking off a coat I'm not wearing.

*Where are you going?*

*Having words.*

*Babe, it was nothing.*

She says *babe* so casual, like we're a couple of ten years rather than a first date.

*I can't let people disrespect you.*

I head on over but she catches my wrist and pulls it. Her strength

30

makes me topple, and I realise I might not be in fighting form. I look over at the lads and decide to let this one slide.

I decide to give them a pass.

*It's okay*, she says.

Again, her face has an emotion and an expression that I just can't read.


## 'Girls' by Moments & Whatnauts

At the next bar, Collette returns from the ladies' looking happy.

She's well caught up on the booze by now. She's on board. We're on the same level. She's drunk too. She whirls across the dance floor. Her mad laugh is glorious, infectious. Her laugh tumbles into my laugh. My hands hold her forearms as we dance. I've ordered a double of something. We slam it hard and dance another dance before ordering again.

*You really ARE drunk*, she shouts through the music.

*I know.*

*Lightweight!*

*Heavyweight!*

These moments feel bulletproof, invincible, unbeatable, a bubble.

For some reason, I keep hurling compliments her way ... *exotic, effervescent.*

*You ... exude.*

*You're a good dancer*, she says, *and a good kisser.*

We dance. We kiss.

We kiss for a long time, so long and so raw, like dumb teenagers oblivious to the outside world.

I move us through the gears, from light and playful to sweet and sensuous to deep and erotic, and then back again.

*Damn*, she says as we separate, breathless.

We're seated now, away from everything. *I like your jawline*, she says, running a finger along my face.

*I think we should make a go of it*, I say.

*What?*

*I think we should make a go of it*, I repeat.

*Yeah?* She laughs softly at this, a little dazed by it all.

Her face is so close that all I can see is a blur of fuzzy pink.

We move on. Out one door and through another. Now the bars and the people behind them become a carousel of nameless, faceless things. Where are we and where are we going? Top of Hockley, rounding the Lace Market. Maybe Ha! Ha! Bar, perhaps Quilted Llama. We are sat on a sofa when a song I know and recognise but haven't heard in ages comes on and lifts me to my feet. I spin on my heels and belt the lyrics right into the face of Collette.

*Girls ... I like 'em fat, I like 'em tall ... some skinny, some small, I got to get to know them all ...*

There is a black guy next to me and I step into his rhythm. Dancing around black people always makes me a better dancer. I pull my head in like a cobra and half-robot myself back towards the seated Collette, belting more of the song's lyrics into her face.

*Love the things they know ... love the things they show ... got to be where they go ... pretty girls ...*

I kiss her forehead and then turn back to the smiling black guy, who now dances with his black girlfriend. They let me join in and the three of us work the floor.

Back to Collette.

More lyrics:

*I'd like to be on an island ... with five or six of them fine ones ... even the ones that ain't good-lookin' ... they're the ones that do the best cookin'.*

Collette turns away from the next kiss, and it's the first time I realise there might be something wrong.

Back to the black couple, clapping and lunging in unison, and the rest of the dance floor watches us, forming a ring, whoopin' and hollerin', joining in. Now the whole floor moves as one.

Back to Collette.

The last of the lyrics:

*Super fine ... mighty fine ... sugar and spice ... everything nice.*
YOU'RE A FUCKING DICK.

She pelts past me, almost knocking me to the floor. I try to track her but get lost in the tangle of people. I stumble and scan, searching everywhere. After a good fifteen minutes I find her at the side of the bar, necking something.

Her face falls in the purple dark.

*Collette.*

I touch her arm but she withdraws.

*What's up?*

*You're a fucking dick*, she says again, not as loud but with much more venom.

*What I do?*

*Girls.*

*What?*

*It's what you've been saying all night ... girls, girl, girls. We're not girls; we're fucking wom-men!*

*It's just a song.*

*I'm not talking about the song; I'm talking about you!*

*I don't—*

*All night I've been biting my lip, but I've had enough.*

*I don't know what you're talking about.*

*Girls. Dear. Darling. BABE.*

*Eh?*

*And it's not just the words but your whole dismissive attitude.*

*What?*

*Your whole COMPLACENT attitude.*

*Collette ...*

*Way you look at us, way you talk about us.*

*Look ...*

*If only you knew.*

*Knew what?*

*Way you talked about my scars earlier. Big fucking hero.*

*I don't remember.*

*And my weight.*

*I was complimenting you.*

*Oh, you're so open-minded.*

*Collette ...*

*Like you're doing ME a favour by taking this date. Showing the world how progressive you are.*

*Collette, this is fucking insane ... I thought we were having a good—*

*But what gets me most is just how unaware you are. Like, even now, that look on your dumb face. So symptomatic of your privilege and the way you move around in the world. That's why I didn't fucking tell you what I'm studying at uni cos it's that look I'd get. That look you're doing NOW. That arrogant, abusive, passive-aggressive bullshit.*

I'm trying to listen but there's some erratic movement bothering my peripheries, in the background. It's then I notice the cavegirls from earlier, the ones at the beginning of the night, The

33

Cornerhouse escalators. They are falling about all over the place, laughing, screaming, pointing. On a closer look, I see they have surrounded two boys, bespectacled geeky-looking lads about the same age. They stand stiff with terror, their hands tight in their pockets. The cavegirls take it in turns to bash them with their inflatable clubs. One of the boys, especially, he is trying to speak to the ringleader. For a while, she seems to take him seriously, giving him her time. She puts her head to one side, taking him in with her eyes. I recognise the smile and the cute wrinkling of the nose she gave me earlier. She laughs at his jokes, head back, exposing her slender throat and the pert pair of solid tits underneath. He's quite taken with her. He's quite hypnotised. Just when he seems to be getting somewhere, she nods to her mate, who then belts him around the tab. Then another cavegirl attacks him from another angle. As the boy pivots to face one cavegirl, he is bashed by another. He ends up spinning around, disorientated and humiliated. He tries to laugh it off, showing he can take it, but he's clearly distressed. What's more, his mate, talking to another cavegirl, tries to get in on the joke, siding with the cavegirl he is standing with; only eventually he gets the same, a belt full in the face. After a few more minutes, all the cavegirls really let loose and launch a full-scale assault on both boys. It's like watching two dopey buffaloes being ravaged by a pack of hyenas. Eventually, the bouncers have to come down and calm it all, but still the boys won't leave. They stick around. While ever there's a promise of something, a whiff of something, they'll take this all night, for the rest of their lives if they have to.

*You're not even listening, are you?*

Sensing my train of concentration has been lost, Collette turns to see the half-naked eighteen-year-olds and loses her shit completely.

*I rest my fucking case.*

For a moment, I feel like she is about to slap me across the face. She even raises her hand but stops herself at the last minute.

*JUST. FUCK. YOU.*

She heads off but this time I don't chase, drink my drink instead and watch more of the scenes around me.

Ringleader Cavegirl is now going at it on the black bouncer. Her face is so different from the escalators, that clear-eyed, freckle-fresh face of vibrancy and mischief. Now she wears a melting mask, something malevolent, something from a Goya painting. One eye is unusually bigger than the other. She spits and snarls, clawing at everything in front of her. The bouncer is reluctant to do anything even though he is being physically attacked. Eventually, a woman bouncer pounds into her from nowhere, rag-dolls her without effort, dragging her up the stairs by her hair, out the door.

The rest of the cavegirls follow, screaming things like, *My mother is a barrister. She'll have this place closed down in a week.*

Through my inebriation, a glow of satisfaction moves through my body at watching this sequence.

I stand for another ten minutes. I stand for another twenty.

My vision is doubling. Acid reflux is building.

Think maybe it's time I bounced.


## Goodbye, Collette

Outside, the church spire of Pitcher & Piano towers in the blue-black sky. The hour is late and the streets are emptying. Black cabs pull up and away with drunken couples, lads, girls. I try to work out what day it is and figure it's around midweek.

Then to my surprise a big blonde blur steps out from a wall.

*Collette.*

She doesn't say anything at first. Her eyes are black and her face is streaked and her jaw is tight and she appears paler in skin tone.

*Hey, you all right?* I ask.

I can't remember anything distinct, only a vague feeling that something has gone wrong, somewhere.

Still no words, just silently tracking me back up towards the top of Hockley.

*So what's the story gonna be to your audience then?*

*My audience?*

*Suppose I'm just going to be that unhinged GIRL, right? Emotionally unstable. The basket case. I mean, that's the portrait you'll paint to your friends, right? The drunken nutter who self-harms and kicks off out the blue.*

*Collette, can we just—*

*All told by the lovable rogue,* she continues, *the cheeky chappy, the harmless raconteur. Only I don't find it lovable, and I certainly don't find it harmless.*

After all this drinking, I'm amazed at the power and clarity of her speech.

At this point, I can barely string a sentence together.

*See, that's how men like you get your misogyny to slip under the radar, nicely and neatly packaged by wink-wink, boys-will-be-boys anecdotes.*

I kick the kerb and almost drop.

*But you know what! I don't even blame you, personally.*

Good. Does this mean—

*Recycled from the patriarchy. Re-recycled from your father and his father. From school and the workplace. Not to mention all the other bullshit I've heard from you tonight. Your unconscious casual racism.*

What?

*Black people being good dancers, catching a PAKI cab, going for a CHINKY, and I'm sure that bouncer REALLY appreciated you calling him BROTHER.*

*Nah. Nah, look ... you don't get it.*

*Oh, save it, Robin. Tell it to your chavvy mates.*

*See, you just, you just—–*

*I'm off.*

And she was, is.

A black cab appeared from nowhere, as if on cue. Door open, lighting up the interior like a spaceship.

*And one more thing ...* her face takes on a new serious sadness, almost like she's nervous all of a sudden, and indeed I notice a lump in her throat. *It takes more than a drunken night before you can ... before we can ... make a go of it ... with someone, with me.*

I grab at her for one last kiss. Her breath is bittersweet, an overwhelm of alcohol and half-hearted lust.

Collette scrunches her eyes and pushes me hard in the chest. It hurts.

She steps in and slams the door and the lights go out.


## Bar Schnapps

I decide I'm not done. And when people decide they're not done, at 2am, 3am, they go to Bar Schnapps. The cobbled road of St James's Street. Laughter behind the large lighted window, tattooed with a swirl of blue handwritten neon *bar schnapps*.

Fuck knows what I order.

Probably a double vod and Red Bull at this achy hour. The

mirror shows my eyes half closed and a hand in the pocket, shirt half tucked in, like a sleepy schoolboy.

Then my name called out.

*Robin!*

I turn to look up the narrow wooden bar. An ominous figure looming at the end of it, a small entourage around him.

*Robin, you cunt!*

Next to him are some rough but highly fuckable women in their forties and a big bruising slab of a thug who is half out of it. Also swarming around him is a pair of dangerous little runts, sniffed-up and dead-eyeing me as I stumble on over, eager to please Vic by so much as a nod.

*Steady on, lads*, Vic says.

The runts step off and disperse.

*Robin, you cunt*, he says again.

He holds me in the glare of his wild green eyes, that gold-capped, gappy-tooth grin.

*You get that fing done?*

Fuck knows what he's on about, but I nod my head anyway.

*Nice one*, he says, stuffing my pocket with a handful of notes. *Might have another little run for you again next week.*

Again, I nod.

*Mr. Brightside* by The Killers plays through the bar. Never did like this song.

*Fuck's that on your lips?* Vic says.

My hand instinctively goes there and when I pull it back, there is gloss on my fingertips.

Brightside song lyrics: *It was only a kiss; it was only a kiss.*

*Aw, looks like he's been on a date*, one of the women says.

*Fuckin' hope that's what it is*, snarls Vic.

From inside this spinning near-mute cocoon I'm in, I feel a sudden stab of loss.

*Bit out of it, hey, kiddy*, Vic says, clicking his fingers around my tabs.

*I'm all right*, I mumble.

*Kid!* My face gets a slap and pain shoots into my eyes, waking me up. *Robin!*

I look up to see a more vivid picture of Vic, raising his glass, the faded swallow inked between his thumb and forefinger flying up to his mouth.

*Fink you need to get yasen home, duck.*

I'm nodding.

*Fink you need to get yasen gone.*

*Yeah*, I manage. *Yeah, you're right.*

I drain my drink and turn on my feet and go to leave Bar Schnapps as the final lines of the song push me out the door.

*I never.*

*I never.*

*I never.*

*I never.*


## Whycliffe

*Can I sing you a song?*

Pigeons explode from the Market Square. The sound of beating wings roars over my head. There is a black face before me. Kind of a familiar one, kind of a famous one.

Cracks of handsomeness shimmer through his crackhead mask.

*Can I sing you a song*? he says again.

His eyes are speedily scanning me, like he's trying to make up his mind about something.

*Whycliffe.* I miraculously pull his name out of my scrambled skull. *Sup?*

*Yes, man.* He gives me a big-fist, a new hope in his eyes. *Yar, ya got change, bro?*

It's probably rare that Whycliffe runs into someone who is in a worse state than him, but this is what he's dealing with right now.

I take out my wallet but there is nothing there. With this, Whycliffe gives his teeth a quick kiss and heads off, towards a small gang of lads up the road.

Heading in that direction, I slowly track his junky shuffle, watching his gait as he pulls away from me.

He reaches the lads and I hear the murmur of his line: *Can I sing you a song?*

There is laughter and mockery, a splash of southern accents, and I know they're not from Nottingham. Everyone knows Whycliffe, yet this is new to them. I have them down as students or a stag do.

*Fackin' 'ell, mate. Hahahahaha.*

Stepping closer, my ear picks up Whycliffe's soulful yet broken tones, a mumble.

*Fackin' speak up, son.*

They're all standing under the blue of Barclays Bank.

Whycliffe tries, a hint of his natural talent but still barely audible.

Next, they get him dancing. *Dance.*

Whycliffe bobs up and down, his feet tippy-tapping along the tramlines.

*Moonwalk*, one of them yells, mid-laughter.

With effort, Whycliffe turns and attempts the backwards movement.

*Yo!*

It's me. My voice perforates the scene. Four sets of eyes snap at me. Whycliffe is still mumbling and moonwalking to himself.

*Yo, you need to show this man some respect.*

I'm right up to them.

*You don't know who this man is, do you? Outside of the Xylophone Man, my man Whycliffe is the most famous celebrity tramp we have.*

The lads look dumfounded.

*Fackin' what?*

*Tell 'em, Whycliffe.*

Whycliffe stops still, blinking and twitching, not knowing what the fuck is going on.

I wipe my mouth. *This man is more than you pricks.*

The lads look at each other.

I step forward and make sure I speak to all of them:

*Song in the charts, toured with James Brown, even shagging Dannii Minogue at one point, wasn't ya, Cliffe?*

Whycliffe mumbles to himself, staring at the boys. *Seen, man. Bless, man.*

I can't really see faces, just pinkish dots of brown and blond.

*Funny, that*, Ringleader points to one of his mates, *cos he was in the charts too, number one hit, toured with Michael Jackson and was shagging her sister, Kylie, for a bit.*

Belting laughter wakes the street up. I notice the first crack of light in the sky.

*Go on, ya lanky streak of piss, fack off!*

Whycliffe has already gone, and no one seems to notice. All eyes on me.

Not scared of these pricks, I take another step forward. There is no adrenalin or nerves, just a clear sight of what I need to do. Ringleader's features now gather before me; a forehead, a set of eyes, a nose and a chin.

It is this chin I'll take.

Feel my fist form.

A little instructive bit of dialogue runs through my head.

*Line up leader and take him out. Once that's done, his pussy mates will back right off because ...*


## Sparko

The bouncing of my bonce against the kerb wakes me back up ... I think. Do I think? Am I thinking? Am I thinking, right now? Are these thoughts that I am thinking? And who do the thoughts belong to, I think, as I think? The age-old Cartesian conundrum as I lay sparko in a pile of bin bags outside Barclays Bank. The sharp sting of urine enters my being; so does the sound of fading laughter. Next, there is another sound. The sound of a tram. A tram-sound of a bell and heavy machinery, moving right towards me, up over me, through me. Then there is a feeling rather than a sound. A feeling of fear. Real, raw, overwhelming fear. Next, there is a death-feeling. A death experience. I am experiencing death. Wait. Nothing. No more tram sound. No more fear feeling. No more death experience. Just silence. Maybe this is all in my head?

Wait. Fuck. Am I dead?

Is this death?

I try to open my eyes and move but nothing.

Just dark. Just black. Just nothingness.

But I'm still experiencing nothingness, so it can't be nothingness.

?

!

?

Wait.

A sound.

I hear a sound.

I hear a sound outside of myself.

A sound that doesn't belong to me.

Outside of these thoughts, outside of this death.

Outside of this experience of being *sparko*.

It's footsteps. It's heels.

It's the clear sound of high heels sparking against the metal of tramlines.

The sound sounds musical, glorious.

It sounds divine.

My eyes open and light pours through them.

Life pours through them.

This is life so I must be alive.

A sideways scene of a woman walking towards me.

A tall blonde angel.

All hips and curves and perfume.

It enters my being and maybe I've died after all.

She bends down and picks me up.

Her strength is supernatural.

I am weightless.

I am wind.

I am air.


Her beautiful face before me. Her dark eyes and her perfect nose.

Her soft lips and the softer, softest voice I've ever heard, saying my name,

*Fuck's sake, Robin.*

Day Two

# The Life

'The road to excess leads to the palace of wisdom.'

William Blake

# Made Marianne

Her dick is bigger than mine.

She's taller too, heavier.

She once beat me in an arm wrestle, and I'm kind of in love with her.

There is a white cloud wrapping me with white arms. Soft strength.

I have gone back into the womb.

I feel this safe bliss for about another five minutes until she at last lets go of me. One arm, then the next arm.

*I gotta go work,* she says.

I hear her move around the apartment, softly, as gentle as she can go.

Maybe I fall asleep again. Cos there seems to be some time that has passed. She is stood before me at the foot of the bed. Fashioned up to the eyeballs in top-notch clobber. A Louis Vuitton wrapped by her long fingers, tight into her shoulder. Her hair is black now, jet black and cut to a short severe bob, like Uma Thurman in *Pulp Fiction.*

*I gotta go work,* she says again.

A distant hell-feeling starts to gnaw at the centre of my psyche.

*Don't worry, I'm not gonna make you get up* … she purrs … *not gonna make you be seen with me in public, in broad daylight* … that second sentence was a mumble and I barely make it out … *I'll leave you here* … her accent that I've never been able to put my finger on … *I hate anyone being here, but I don't think you could stand even if I made you.* Her eyes are bright black, bottomless and doe-like. Her nose belongs to high society. It flares with pomposity whenever she says certain words. *I've made you breakfast. It's in the microwave. There's OJ in the fridge and I've put some paracetamol next to you.*

I try to turn my head but can't.

*You're gonna need them.*

Marianne bends to adjust her boot.

I manage words at last: *what, where, time I come here last night?*

*This morning,* Marianne corrects sharply. *And you didn't come here, I found you.*

*Found me?*

*Luckily, I found you.*

*What?*

*You were lying in trash. Your leg over the tramline.*

*Whoa.*

*Your foot would have been decapitated.*

This makes me smile somehow although Marianne is deadly serious.

*I think someone hit you and I think someone kissed you.*

*Eh?*

*There was a mark on your face and gloss on your lips.*

Now her hurt attitude makes sense.

And the slight ache in my jaw.

*Maybe the two are related, but who knows and who cares.*

I'm staring into space.

*You don't remember?*

I shake my head. *I don't remember a thing.*

Marianne shakes hers now. *I don't know why you do this to yourself.*

*Where was I?*

*In town, near Waterstones.*

*Wait. You carried me all the way from Waterstones, near Barclays? And up two flights of stairs?*

She turns the other way and drops her head, embarrassed.

*It had to be done,* she says finally. *Anyway, I'm late for work now and I hate being late.*

She clutches her Louis tighter and heads towards the door.

*Marianne.*

*What?*

She still has her head down.

*Let's do something tonight.*

She doesn't say anything.

*Let's go out tonight?*

*You're still drunk,* she says.

*I mean it. You saved my life ... well ... my foot ... I owe you.*

A smile now. *You owe me nothing.*

*Time you back?*

*Seven.*

*Time is it now?*

*Twelve. And I'm LATE.*

She opens the door.

*We'll go out. I'll take you out. Dinner.*

She closes the door and lifts her head and turns to me, stands tall. She smiles fully for the first time of the day. Her beauty is not quite real.

*I don't quite believe it but I accept it, for now.*

I nod.

*Please, don't snoop*, she says.

*I won't.*

*Promise. I'm deadly serious about this.*

*I promise. I won't.*

She goes to leave.

*Marianne.*

*Yes.*

*Thank You.*

She looks warmly at me; something so knowing and tender passes between us as she steps out of her apartment.

*And, Marianne…*

Her voice echoes in the stairwell. *Fuck's sake, Robin, just let me go!*

Cocks her head back round the door. *What?*

*Did we … do owt last night?* I say.

I am kneeling naked on the bed, pressing her pillow into my rib.

She leans in a little, spying through a peephole in the covers.

*You wish.*


## Eternal Recurrence

We've all had this at some point in our lives. But I've had it worse. Right now. Right now, I am having it worse than the lot of you, all of you out there. By a country mile. Marianne was right; I was still drunk. Because what happens in the next hour is nothing less than evil. Pure, uncomplicated evil. I fall into full hangover. I crash into a screaming mess. My skull shatters. This is utter chaos. I try to get up and I try to get up. Each time I do, I collapse back into the white mass of the duvet, as if someone has swiped my legs from under me. When I do finally manage the walk across the hall, daylight slashes at me from all angles. The morning uses a knife. I walk into walls and stub my toe. Into the glaring white of that spinning bathroom. I paint the toilet with several coats of vomit, proper projectile vomit.

This marathon vomiting goes on for so long and is so violent I actually consider ringing three 9s. I spit and whimper and almost cry as I'm doubled up over the polluted waters, watching my own shadowy reflection lurk in the murky depths.

I am infected. I am rotten.

Next is the headache. Not a headache but migraine. An army of lemmings dig through my skull. Going to work with hammers and a pickaxe. Blocking, bombing, building and bashing. Sling a rope around my brain and yank it full force. In and around the eye sockets. Drilling down through the roof.

Nothing else exists outside of this pain. The whole cruel world is in my head.

I will never do this to myself again, I vow.

I will never do this to myself again, I repeat.

The mantra becomes its own madness, and I wonder if I've fallen into the inescapable loop of psychosis.

After a good hour chained to this cold bathroom floor I carry myself back to bed and drop right in it. When I no longer feel the threat of sicking them back up, I pop the paracetamol.

Maybe sleep.

Maybe nightmare.

I hear voices and have visions, flashbacks from the night before.

Cavegirl on her knees before me. Her beautiful, demotic face. Eyes closed. Mouth open. The pink of her tongue, held between her straight white teeth, before slowly sliding it through her lips. Closer and closer. She opens her eyes and looks at me, that wrinkling of the nose. Only to pull away at the last moment, belting my cock with her club, laughing dementedly as it shrinks back through a tiny hole in my stomach ... More images move on a reel ... Vic and his entourage ... *You get that fing done for me, Robin?* Whycliffe on the street, big-eyed and frightened and lost, the faceless lads who put me on my arse, cheering and jeering as Whycliffe and me try and moonwalk for them. *Dance.* Then black. Then white. Then black again. An oncoming tram moves through it. Sound of a bell loud in my ear. The metallic beast screeches and I soundlessly scream as it runs over my legs.

I wake and gasp, panting. Marianne's bedroom slowly reforms, returning me to reality. My head is still going with last night.

Everything from last night. Everything but the girl.

The person I went on a date with.

I no longer remember her face.
I no longer remember her name.

A smaller dreamless sleep.

When I wake for real, I feel marginally better. Taking tentative sips from the glass of water Marianne placed next to my sleeping head. I stretch and roll.

When I can at last manage my phone, I see several texts and three missed calls from

## Cassidy

*Robin.*
*Cassidy.*
*Robin, fank fuck.*
*Yeah.*
*What happened?*
*What do you mean, what happened?*
*How did it go?*
*It went.*
*Fucked it up, dint yar?*
*Not now, Cass.*
*Knew it.*
*Knew what?*
Her dogs are barking in the background.
*Where are yar anyway?*
I look up at a framed picture of Marianne, burlesque model shoot, bursting cleavage, open mouth.
*You don't wanna know.*
*What the fuck does that mean?*
*Nowt.*
*Got banged up, dint yar?*
*Yeah, cos feds allow phones in cells these days.*
*What?*
*Cells in cells.*
*What?*
*Nowt.*
*Got banged out, dint yar?*
I touch the bruising on my chin. It was a love-tap, at best.

*Look, Cassidy, you've heard my voice. You know I'm alive. Can I go now?*

*Knew it.*

*Knew what?*

*Ya hungover ta fuck.*

*Yes, I had a little drink. That's what people do on dates; they drink.*

*She fucked you off, dint she?*

I move the phone from one ear to the other.

*Maybe I fucked her off.*

*Yeah ... right.*

*Can I go now, Cassidy?*

*Honestly, Robin, where are yar?*

*Home.*

*Liar.*

*I am.*

*I'll come round and check then.*

*Agoraphobic's day out?*

*I'll get someone to come round and check then.*

*Don't you need friends for that?*

*FUCK YOU.*

A painful pause steps in between us.

She breaks it. *Time you got work?*

The pain returns.

The pain multiples.

The hangover quadruples.

A sudden dread so breathtaking I physically wince.

The prospect of the day fades away, the dinner date with Marianne and my promise to her falls through, the potential of recovery by way of—

*You better go.*

*Where?*

*Your job, you better go.*

*I know, I will.*

*Last warning.*

*Don't I know it!*

*Lose this job and you're fucked.*

*Cassidy.*

*What?*

*Lend us twenty?*

*Fuck off.*

*I get paid tomorrow.*

*No way.*

*It's only twenty quid.*

*It's not the twenty quid; it's what you'll do with it.*

*What will I do with it?*

*Turn it to liquid.*

*What?*

*Straight to the off-licence.*

*Nah.*

*I'm not being an enabler, Robin.*

*Fuck you talking about?*

*I won't enable you, Robin.*

*Why do you keep saying my name?*

*I knew this would happen.*

*What?*

*One little date and you're back on it.*

*Nah.*

*Probably the only reason you went on the date in the first place.*

I turn this notion over in my brain for a second.

*You better go work.*

*I will.*

*Piece-of-piss job anyway. All ya gotta do is sit with a retard and watch telly.*

*Bit like coming over to your house.*

*Fuck you.*

*Oh.*

*Easier than your last job.*

*Those wop-fucks still owe me two hundred quid.*

*Fat chance of getting that.*

*They owe me.*

*After you banged out all their windows?*

*They don't know that.*

*Doesn't take a scientist.*

*What you mean?*

*Sacked on the Friday, windows go through on the Saturday.*

*Yeah, well.*

*Doesn't take Sherlock Holmes.*

*Well, yeah.*

*Still can't believe you did that.*

*I don't remember it.*

*Yeah, well, you did, cah Neal told me.*

*How the fuck does he know?*

*Cos he was there, you bellend. Did it with you, ya moron.*

*Well, I don't fucking remember.*

*Twats.*

*Yeah, well, I still want my two hundred.*

*You need to be careful. You know those Italians are connected.*

*It's Carlton, Cassidy, not Brooklyn.*

*It started by you tryna tap their youngest daughter, the waitress.*

*Luna.*

*Yeah, her.*

*Damn, she was hot.*

*Not worth losing a job over. That's your trouble, Robin. You're cunt-mad. Gets you in just as much trouble as the booze.*

*You going to lend me that twenty or what?*

*No.*

*Ten then?*

*No.*

*I'm off.*

*So am I.*

*Later, slag.*

*Later, prick.*

## Salma & Jennifer

I'm still tingling from the dream. I feel uncomfortable down there, tender down here. This is another thing about the hangover. Any guy will tell you. The debilitating, all-consuming rage of horniness. It swells as the hangover thins. It becomes a fixation, a fanaticism. *The* fanaticism. The only thing that there is. It is not a want, but a *need*. In the hierarchy of them, it lives next door to food and sleep. Maslow knew fuck all. Hungover and horny. *Hornover.* He never put that one in his book. It moves beyond free will. It has a life of its own. It decides for you without so much as a consultation or check-in. It doesn't just decide for you but often *against* you.

The Devil has other plans.

I need to get rid of this before it does some serious damage.

I need to get rid of this before it gets rid of me.

The nearest thing I see is the framed picture of Marianne on the wall, burlesque model shoot, bursting cleavage, open mouth.

Only either side are other framed pics. Pics with pecs. Two twisting torsos of muscled gladiators.

*Fuck that.*

Instead, I go search for something else.

Catch a pathetic sight of myself in the full-length: naked, skin-thin, ill-white. A semi-on slapping modestly between my bony thighs.

I am stooped and lopsided.

Hideous and horrendous.

A hunchback, craving like a fiend. Like a crackhead in search of a rock.

I go through Marianne's drawers, cupboards.

What I'm looking for, I don't know.

At last, I find her DVD collection. I rifle through it.

A tasteless load of shit. Musicals and romcoms.

At last, I find what I'm looking for.

At last, I find the antidote to this sickness.

At last, I find Salma.

It's good because obvious porn has never done much for me. Nothing left for the imagination. I've always preferred real actresses in real films. A twenty-second window, a look through the keyhole and then fantasy does the rest of the work. Real actresses who appear in other films, other worlds.

Women we come to know. Women we build relationships with.

Halle Berry, *Monster's Ball.*

Helen Mirren, *Caligula.*

Madonna, *Body of Evidence.*

Sharon Stone, *Basic Instinct.*

Jamie Lee Curtis, *Trading Places, True Lies.*

Jennifer Lopez, *U-turn.*

The girls getting it on with each other in *Wild Things.*

The girls getting it on with each other in *Cruel Intentions.*

Natalie Portman and Mila Kunis in the future.

Anything with Marisa Tomei over the age of forty.

Julie Walters under the age of thirty.

Julia Roberts in 1990.

Bo Derek. Pam Grier.

The golden age of cinema.

The Hepburns. Hayworth. Harlow. Bardot.

Sophia Loren.

I take *From Dusk Till Dawn* out of the case and load it into the player. Only I haven't got a clue how to turn this bastard telly on and in a sudden moment the hangover returns like a boomerang and sticks in the back of my head. For a minute, I think I might be sick again.

I touch my chest.

I hold it down.

At last, by a miracle, I get the TV on. The film's menu page up on the big screen. I feel feverish with lust, out of my mind with frustration that Marianne isn't here. I contemplate holding off until she comes back. I contemplate dropping her a text, see if she wants to pop back for some late lunch. I'm aware that I'm selfishly using her for my needs.

Or ... do girls like that feel used in the same way?

Surely they know what it's like.

Surely they can *empathise*.

This cock 'n' bull story.

The curtain parts and Salma steps out. Men howl in the crowd. There is a neon red flame behind her. She flaps her cape like a bat. She wears a feathered crown on her head. The music starts. Cool, visceral music. The stage goes up in flames. A yellow snake crawls through her curves. Men sit in the shadows. A shot of her smooth brown buttocks. Arches her back and rolls her hips. The band plays on. *In her eyes, a distant firelight burns bright, wondering, if it's only after dark.* She works the snake and the snake tries to work her. She steps down towards us. She walks over glass. Guitar strums, aches. She pours alcohol down herself and licks it off her foot. She sets her hair free, long raven hair, tousled, everywhere. The scene reaches its climax as I reach mine.

Achieving this mini-death through the obliterating oblivion of O.

Gestalt Cycle complete, until the next time.

After a minute or two, there is that *what was all the fuss about?*

What's the big deal?

Almost aloof in the face of lowly lust, and its repetitious

properties. The hedonic treadmill. Siding myself with the Stoics. Wouldn't get Seneca doing this shit. Aurelius or Epictetus.

Now out of the system, I share a seat with Plato and his Philosopher Kings.

I clean up and return to the DVD collection. Fingering through the titles, but there's not much here. The chance of any sophisticated cinema is zilch, so instead I feel for something cosy and nostalgic. The post-masturbatory feeling of shame still hangs, so I search for something pure of heart, something to remind me of when life was simple and clean.

At last, I find her.

*Labyrinth.*

I take out Salma and replace her with Jennifer.

Catch myself in the full-length again and notice that I am curled up and clutching the cushion like a six-year-old with his favourite teddy bear.

Haven't watched this film in years, and it shocks me that I fall right back in love with Jennifer as soon as she appears on the screen. The feeling is weird. I cringe at the nonceyness of it. But the more I sit, the more I feel the *sweetest feeling*, desire-free. First crush in the playground. I remember seeing somewhere that Jennifer and I share the exact same birthday, only she is ten years older than me. 1970, 1980. She was fifteen when this film was made and I was five. Back then, I remember thinking how adult and heroic she was. Entering the fantastical labyrinth to save her baby brother from the clutches of evil. Now she is still fifteen and I am twenty-seven. I watch her through my adolescent eyes.

All this ageing and passing of time makes me feel emotional, and I realise how lost I am.

In the end, the goblins freak me out, the *Bog of Eternal Stench* makes me want to hurl and David Bowie just stalks about like a slimy nonce, so I decide to shut this whole thing down.

## The Bottle

Marianne's studio apartment; white, silver and fluffy.

I'm not hungry, just as I never am, but suppose something should go in the system. Check the breakfast. Don't reheat it, just grab at bits as I go.

Stuff a sausage in my mouth. Lick fat off the bacon.

Poke the yoke of an egg.

I can't taste flavour.

Fuck, I'm still hungover, and a second wave of it washes through me. I'm sick again. Not as violent as earlier but my body is still set against me. Once my head clears, the logical world of chronological time, of one thing leading to another thing, begins to appear before me. *Work.* I have work tonight. A clock on the wall tells me I have work in six hours' time. The evening shift where I, in Cassidy's words, *sit with a retard and watch telly.* This may sound easy but it's not. There's handover with the day staff and my boss to face. I have to make dinner. I have to take phone calls.

I have to wipe an arse.

Marianne has left a window open and there is a faint wind-whooshing of the trees, against the distant hum of traffic. I close my eyes and tune in.

A dog bark. A church bell. A bump from next door. A cough. A boy saying, *Mum.* A sparkle of wind chimes in my mind's eye. For a sober moment, the afternoon has perfect clarity. I feel fine, free of craving. I shall take this state home with me, I muse. I shall leave Marianne a loving note, informing her I have work. I shall write warm words on paper, thanking her, telling her how I cherish her care and will return in a few days, on my day off, to take her out for a real meal. No drinking; just a proper, proper date.

Yes, this is what I am going to do.

I look for a pen.

I pull drawers, search shelves. I move things.

I put things back. I ransack.

How can a whole apartment not have a pen?

All of a sudden, my zen gets soiled by stress.

Really, I should simply send her a text, just like the 2008 that it is, but the romanticism of a handwritten note is a piece of poetry I can't miss.

I search. I search and search and still nothing.

I'm opening all the cupboards, and I'm opening them quite aggressively by now.

I'm shouting out to myself. I'm slamming. I pull at every handle in the joint, and that's when I open the fridge and that's when I'm stopped dead in my tracks, dead in my socks, dead in my life

because my breath stops and my eyes slam on a big bright bottle, gleaming in the centre of the fridge. Golden.

If I wasn't so speechless I'd say *Fuck.*

I take it out without really thinking. Ripping at the expensive label. Shards of gold twirl and tickle my kneecaps as they drop to the floor. The brown eye of a cork. I wedge two thumbs under it. Don't think I've ever opened a bottle of champagne before. It's hard. It's tricky. I feel a deathly desperation that something might go wrong. That I'll fuck it up somehow and imprison the alcohol *for life.*

POP.

Thud against the ceiling.

Champagne doing what champagne does. I catch most of it in my mouth and straight away the world gets right again. I swallow fast and swallow hard. Hobbling over to the sink so as not to spill it on the floor.

Slower sips.

After about five tugs, the hangover dies.

Like pouring boiling water over ice, I watch it melt away.

Literally dissolve –

Migraine, gone. Sickness, gone.

Nausea, gone. Confusion, gone.

Self-doubt, gone. Inadequacy, gone.

Shakes, gone. Aches, gone.

Like Popeye slinging spinach down his gob, I bulge and pop.

I walk the room, drinking coolly from the bottle.

I feel how free I am.

How amazing I am.

How I always land on my feet. How I shine.

My adventures are iconic.

My style is legendary.

I wonder what the day will bring.

## Peacocking

The billowy April streets slide on by, glide on by. I scratch my armpit and realise I've not showered. This is not a good sign. Already that myopia, of neglecting human necessities, like splashing a face and brushing the tegs.

I feel glorious, though; there's no doubt about it.

It's only money that is keeping me out of a pub right now. I walk by one of my favourite ones. The Peacock. This is the boozer I use at the very end of my benders. Its cosy interior, soft seats and gentle clientele always bring me down nice, like a slow plane touching down on a long and easy runway. Bitter drinkers. Moderate drinkers. A thinking man's public house. Lecturers, lefties. Board games. A soothing library quiet. Low music, low lighting. Like your nan's living room. People sit in shaded corners and mind their business, yet always an effortless conversation to fall into should you want it. Yes, this is the pub to fix the future with. To prepare the withdrawal with. To smooth off the sharpness of the rattle with half a dozen Guinnesses. It's funny how six pints at the beginning of a bender is getting pissed whereas six at the end is mere medicine. The shelf life and timing and science of drinking. An art form.

The Peacock, the bold font, gold next to green.

Even now, as I pass the open door, a cone of springtime sun reaches through and tugs at my arm.

Just as I meditate on this, I hear my name being called.

Being called once, being called twice, being called a third time.

A figure stepping out from the YMCA.

He looks like a scarecrow against the backdrop of Midlands sky; rigid, bent, weathered and woebegone.

A long face, handsome face – mixed-race, Yorkshire accent up out the earth, calling my name.

I call out his name in return.

## Fry

I don't know where I found him. I don't remember. It could have been an alleyway. The corner of a pub. The street, park bench. He believes I was sent to him by God at the stroke of midnight. Says he was stranded, trying to get on an empty bus, only he didn't have the fare. Says I appeared from nowhere, paid his ticket and looked after him until he got home. Says he was withdrawing and that I helped him with that too. Fry tells me this story again and again.

But, I can honestly say, I haven't got a clue what he's talking about.

He still believes I was sent to him by God. I keep telling him that I have my own life to live and that God has nothing to do with it. Suppose I should leave him to believe what he wants. I give him money when I can, help him out. Only Fry doesn't realise that I need him as much as he needs me. He is a constant companion that is readily available whenever I *slip under*. A 24/7 sidekick.

*Where you been, our kid?*

I tell him but he doesn't really listen. Slurping on the last of his Pot Noodle. That's why he's at the YMCA, to get boiling water for his Pot Noodle. It's a part of his daily routine: Off-licence. Methadone. Drug worker. Raise funds. Back to off-licence. Pot Noodle. Pot Noodle is all he eats. One in the afternoon. One late at night. His tongue is green.

We automatically head up towards the Arboretum. Day weakened as the sun slips behind the skyline mass of the Victoria flats.

I go into full detail about the night as we hobble up Mansfield Road.

*Honestly, Fry, I was all set to come home and sober up, sleep it off and get ready for work … but then I open the fridge and there is a bottle of champagne. It was a sign from God.*

*You don't believe in God.*

Fry still isn't really listening. There's an antagonism to his tone.

*Anyway*, he cuts in, *decided I'm leaving this city. In the next week. Swear on my grandma's grave.*

The bottle of White Storm bulges behind his jacket.

*You say this every week.*

*This time, I mean it.*

*You say that every week too.*

*Going back to Hull, me.*

Fry got let out of HMP Nottingham three years ago. He's been here ever since.

*Swear on my grandma's grave.*

*All right.*

*This fucking city. Dealers won't leave me alone. Ya buyin' from*

*Medders, man? Ya buyin from Stannz, man? I keep tryna tell them ...*
*I'm buyin' from no man. As if tryna kick isn't hard enough, I've got*
*these parasites leeching off me every five minutes. They've even*
*started turning up at my yard. I'm done with this city. Going back to*
*Hull, me. Swear on my grandma's grave.*

Fry is killing my champagne high.

I see something that might take him out of it.

*Hey, Fry, there's your girl*, I say, pointing to a celebrity face on a
newspaper.


## Cheryl Cole

*Aw, she's beautiful, bruv.*

Fry has a thing for Cheryl Cole. In fact, it's a bit more than a thing.
He believes she is his guardian angel. I was his guardian angel, and
Cheryl Cole was his guardian angel. I guess that makes us his
parents. Cheryl is my spiritual wife. Occasionally, I'd wind him up.

*You know who I think is an utter dog?*

*Who?*

*Everyone goes on about her, but I don't know what the big fuss is.*

*Who?*

*Cheryl Cole.*

He would bolt out of whatever slumber he was in.

*Are you off your head?*

*Dog.*

*She's beautiful, bruv.*

It's the only time I see him come alive. Part of the reason I do it.
Put some life back into him. His eyes would go large and he'd form
a fist, defending his queen.

I do this every time I see him. This wind-up. He never
remembers a thing. A lifetime on the gear has completely pickled
his brain.

*I swear on my grandma's grave. She's beautiful, bruv.*

*Nah.*

*It's been proven. She's got the best eyes.*

There was nothing impure about Fry's feelings towards Cheryl.
And that was sweet. Fry, as far as I have witnessed, is completely
devoid of sexual feeling. He is a non-sexual being.

# Arboretum

*My drug worker says the reason I'm feeling like this is cos I'm getting my emotions back.*

We are sitting by the war memorial in the Arboretum, between a set of giant cannons.

*You've done well, Fry. How long you been clean now?*

*Twenty-one days.*

*See,* I say, slapping his chest.

*Not really clean, though, is it? Now I'm on this shit.*

He slaps the White Storm in his jacket and I hear the slosh of liquid.

Amazed I haven't asked for a swallow yet. The champagne is running through my veins. I still feel good.

*To be honest, Robin, think I was better on the rock.*

*Don't say that shit, Fry.*

*It's true, though. Never felt as low as I am now.*

*You just need time, man. Like your drug worker says. Just getting your emotions back.*

Fry swings his head one way, then the other.

*Stay with it,* I say.

His eyes are so wide, innocent and lost. Breaks your heart.

*Tell ya what,* I begin. *There's probably a thirty per cent chance I've been paid. Let's go to a cashpoint, and if I have then we'll get on it. My treat. Straight in the Wethers for a full day on the piss.*

I'm saying this like I'm doing it for *him*. For Fry. An altruistic act.

*Thought you had work, bruv.*

I wave him off.

*Thought you were on your final warning.*

*Forget that shit.*

*Oh, Robin, you're too good to me, bruv.*

I put my arm around him and try to pull him in. Even though he was an alkie/addict. Fucker was strong.

*You're my boy,* I say.

*When I get out of this, I'm paying you back,* he says. *Every penny. Swear on my grandma's grave.*

*Well, let's not get our hopes up. Thirty per cent chance, remember.*

The Arboretum is a pleasure to walk through. Windy paths. Twisty trees. Bold green lawns. Cute café at the bottom. Ducks on water. A big birdcage with a hundred birds singing as we walk on by.


## ATM

*Fuck, I'm nervous.*

The dark reflection of Fry and myself moves around as I take out my card. We look like a set of gruesome Siamese twins.

*Gimmie space.*

*Tut. Don't worry, I'm not gonna fuckin' spy at your pin code.*

*It's not that.*

It is that.

*Fuck's sake, Robin.*

He breaks away and sits on the kerb, mumbling:

*Mean the world to me, bruv, saved my life. Not gonna fuckin' stiff ya. Can't believe you'd think that, bruv ... swear on my grandma's ...*

I'm not listening. Too busy taking in deep breaths. Staring into the face of the ATM. The screen, the slot and the keys. Fry ain't too fussed cos he'll just raise enough for another bottle. Go back to his hole, slurp under the covers. It's just another day for him.

I want pub. I want people. I want noise and magic. I want riot. I want *out*.

And this here machine is going to decide all that in the next two minutes.

Fry is right. I don't believe in God, yet I find my eyes drifting up to the heavens. A sort of mantra coming through my lips as the blue of Barclays is pushed into the machine.

Next, there is noise, like the ATM is having an inner dialogue about my fate:

*Go on then, let's chuck the skinny man a twenty. Give him another day on the piss. He deserves it after all he went through last night.*

*Nah, fuck him*, says the other half. *Let's deny the cunt. Teach him a lesson. Tough love. Prick needs to sober up and go home. Sleep it off. Go work. We'd be doing the arsehole a favour.*

Fry shouts up from the kerb, *Fuck's sake, Robin, how long's it take?*

Options appear on the screen and this is a good sign. Like I've got this far. Jumped one hurdle and on to the next.

I ask for twenty quid. I mean, being paid is being paid. If I have then there should be a couple of hundred in there, but asking for *just twenty* feels like humility.

Oliver fucking Twist.

My stomach cramps and I dribble a bit in my pants. That auspicious spitting sound. Gathering up notes.

In the reflection, I see how serious my face has got. My hand slowly drifting up towards the machine's mouth, waiting for it to cough up dollar.

when
from nowhere
those two words
in solid capitals
emblazoned across the machine's forehead:

## INSUFFICIENT FUNDS

I wanna punch the screen. I wanna break my hand. I wanna take a shard from the broken glass and slice my own throat. All of a sudden, I see the future.

Bus. Home. Bed. Bus. Work. Drudgery.

All of the above as the booze drains out of my body, leaving my being to bathe in a bath of acid.

I drop to the kerb with Fry. Side by side, like we always are. He tips the last of the White Storm through his chalky brown lips. He doesn't say anything cos he doesn't need to say anything cos he knows the outcome. Part of him is probably glad, so he doesn't have to face the crowd. He can go home now. I'm even tempted to go with him. Raise enough for a bottle. Go squat in the stink of his room for the next few days.

He suddenly gets up and starts moving.

For some reason, I put my hand in my jeans pocket. It feels crowded down there. I go in deeper. First my wallet then my phone then my keys. Something else is in there. Way down deep. Down in the depths. I touch it. Feels feathery. I pinch and pull it out.

A wad of notes.

A miraculous wad of notes.

Some fives. Some tens. And a twenty.

The shock that must be on my face as I come eye to eye with several Queen Elizabeths. Breathlessly, I count them out loud.

Fry is just a distant figure on the hill by now.

I shout his name.

Keeps on moving.

I shout his name again.

Stops and looks at me.

*Never gonna believe this.*

*What?*

*I've just found a bullseye in my rocket.*


### The Joseph Else

Wetherspoons on The Square. We enter to a racket. High chairs and high tables. Littered with locals, losers. The keys to the city. The kings of Nottingham. As I head to the bar, I clock which table to pick, which mini-world would work best for today. Still reeling and confused as to where this dollar came from. For the first time ever, entertain the notion that there might be a God up there.

*Two Strongbows, please, baby.*

My favourite bargirl too.

Bang-tidy gothy-thing, with a face full of piercings. Slams down the pints and rolls her dark eyes.

*Keep the change, sweetheart.*

Fry follows, slightly begrudging, and really all he wants to do is get his hands on the booze.

Which now he does. Biting into it like his life depended on it. Which it kind of does.

I look around. Consider the candidates. The company I keep.

I make my selection.

And head towards a table.


### Li'l Ron Wilk, Turkish and Shaun of the Dead

Li'l Ron ain't li'l. He's a monstrosity of a man. Taking up most of the table. Term *tasty cunt* was founded upon Wilk. I've seen him go.

Speed of the man coupled with the size of the man defies physics. Once watched a martial arts expert take a stance, only for Wilk to windmill right through him in about five seconds. Turkish is actually from Tunisia, but calling him *Tunisia* would make him sound like a girl. Turkish is polite, refined and knowledgeable. He's travelled the world but for some reason decided to set up camp in this shithole. Shaun of the Dead does what he says on the tin. He looks like he's on the edge of it, that dug-up quality. Destitute, dizzy and deformed.

In everyday society, these three wouldn't give each other a glance. Their worlds are only joined at this table for one reason.

*Whose fuckin' round is it?*

They are talking about suicide as we take to the table.

Turkish gives Fry and me a courteous nod each. Shaun scans us from the tops of his eyes, wondering where the charity is at. Wilk bare blanks us, more focused on what he is saying.

*Gun. That's gorra be a dead cert. Quick, easy, painless. I'd tek the fuckin' gun.*

*Not at all*, Turkish says. *You hit the wrong part of the brain and you can end up as a cabbage. Imagine that for the rest of your days. Your body dead but your mind still alive. That is a hell on earth, surely.*

*I know what I'd do*, Shaun adds, *I'd take myself up to the roof of Victoria flats. Got to be twenty stories or more. Sure to put you in a coffin, a jump from there.*

Wilk: *Wish you would so I wouldn't have to smell you anymore, ya dirty cunt.*

Shaun moves his grubby hands across his chest.

*What's up with you, man?* Wilk continues, screwing his mouth in disgust. *Ya gerrin' worse.*

*Got nowhere to go, have I?* Shaun says helplessly.

*Well, where did you sleep last night?*

*On the Forest.*

*Fuck's sake. Sort yasen out, youth. I mean, we all like a drink, fucking hell. Turkish, me, Fry over there. But, fella, you've gorra wash.*

I feel a twinge at being left out.

*Am I that bad?* Shaun says.

*Bad*, Turkish coolly affirms.

Wilk pulls his Timberland over his gut. *We're talking about how we'd do ourselves in. One more day out with you would be a fucking suicide itself.*

*What about slitting your wrists?* Fry chirps in.

There's a look on Fry's face that unnerves me.

*Fuck that*, Wilk groans, *ant you ever seen* Scum?

*And even that method is not certain*, Turkish adds, thought lines creasing his forehead.

*What, severing the veins in your wrist, how can that not be certain?*

Turkish gathers his words carefully, before turning them loose:

*Most people make the mistake of thinking that the wrists have to be severed across, from left to right. When, in actual fact, the incision should be made vertically.*

Wilk, exasperated: *Well then, you make it fucking VERTICAL, don't ya.*

*Even then someone could walk in on you.*

*I'd still say Victoria flats*, Shaun pipes up. *Twenty stories! You're bound to snuff it.*

*This is not true*, Turkish says. *Ever hear about that man in Tokyo who jumped from a skyscraper and lived?*

Wilk takes a long pull on his pint. *Must have had a cunting parachute.*

*No, it is true*, Turkish says delicately. *Read up on it. Fifty stories. Broke every bone in his body but survived.*

*Well, there's got to be one way?* Wilk blasts. *Fuck me, Turkish, never known anyone so pessimistic about suicide.*

*Just go Thurland on a Sunday night dressed in a Ku Klux Klan outfit. That'd put you in a grave.*

Laughter bursts from the table.

*That was a good one, Shaun*, Wilk approves. *I'll let you have that.*

Turk doesn't approve. He gets back on topic.

*The only definite method of instant death, I would say, is by train.*

*Uwww, ya cunt!* Wilk guffaws. *Yeah, ya right. Seen the speed of them tubes down London. Head-butting one of those bastards is a one-way ticket, nowt so fucking sure.*

*What about drowning?* Shaun chimes in. *As you go, it's supposed to be quite erotic.*

*Well, what's the point of being erotic when you're fucking dead?*

Me: *I think he means euphoric.*

It's the first time Li'l Ron Wilk acknowledges I'm here.

*Unless you get fucked by a mermaid*, Shaun says.

Another blast of laughter.

Wilk rotates his pint. *How can you get fucked by a mermaid, you divvy cunt? It's got no hole. Hand job, blow job, titwank. That's all ya gerrin' out of that bitch.*

Shaun's eyes brighten. *What about ramming her up the shitter?*

*Are you fucking gormy?* Wilk is starting to get short on temper. *She ant got no shitter, either.*

A far-off mystery mists the eyes of Turkish, slight smile.

*From suicide to the sexual complexities of mermaids*, he contemplates. *Now I know why I drink here.*

### Vic

From nowhere, I know exactly where this money came from. This fifty.

A flashback of a face.

A gappy-toothed, wild-eyed face howling at the moon. Stuffing it in my pocket:

*Get that fing done for me, Robin?*

I shudder. Shit myself proper. Instinctively, I look over my shoulder, scan the pub.

Give it the once-over. The dangerous cunt tucked away in some corner. Hiding behind a newspaper. Obscured by the body of a bruiser, or two.

I sober up for a moment.

### Coupons

Conversation goes on hold as crumpled discount coupons are extracted from pockets and placed on the table.

*Whose fuckin' round is it?*

Shaun of the Dead looks down, full of self-pity. Yet the main description that fits his face is *desperation*. Wilk's thick oil-stained fingers go flicking through the coupons.

*Don't tell me we're out of John Smith's?*

Arching his eyebrows, Turkish flicks through the bits of paper too.

*It appears so*, he says.

Turkish looks most out of place here. It's as if he should be transported back to 1930s Paris. In the Montparnasse district, lounging in a bistro. Sipping coffee while philosophising with Henry Miller. In here, he is just scarred and quizzical. Both reaching out and hanging on at the same time. A true alcoholic in every sense of the word.

*Well, I'm the only cunt who drinks Smith's, so where they all gone?*

*You drank about five pints already*, Turkish informs.

*I've got some left*, Shaun says. Hope lighting his eyes for a second. He hands Wilk a clump of coupons.

*What ya giving them me for? Your round.*

Shaun shows the top of his head as he looks at the floor. A perfect circle of matted grease. A stain of something on his Chatty fleece. Slowly, he turns his eyes up, like an orphan. *Ran out of money, ant I?*

*Cheeky cunt!*

Shaun's lip falls out.

*Sitting there supping with no coin in ya pocket.*

*Nah, we're square, Wilk. Am not in ya debt, honest.*

Wilk's piggy face snarls. *You sure?*

*Honestly, Wilk, I wouldn't take the piss.*

*Turk?*

*He's right*, Turkish says, a quick calculation in his head. *We're five each, square.*

Wilk breathes out and tension lifts from the table. Fry is looking outside, hating every minute of this.

Next, a spiteful smile spreads across Wilk's face.

*That's it then*, he says. *Home time for you.*

Shaun starts to twitch like a dying insect.

*Early shower.* Wilk sniffs twice, hard. *Could fuckin' do with one an' all.*

Shaun starts to eye each of us, one at a time.

*No good looking at us, pal. We've done all we can.*

I feel his pain. I know what he's going through. And there's nothing worse.

He slides a hand around his own neck and pulls.

*Throw us one more ten, Ron. Pay you back, promise.*

Shaun's survival overtakes pub etiquette. Wilk's eyes widen in disbelief.

The rest of us cringe at his audacity.

*Cheeky cunt*, Wilk snaps. *You already owe us a score.*

*A fiver then?* Shaun yelps. His eyes moisten. His mouth becomes so small it seems to disappear.

Wilk half stands, preparing some kind of speech.

*Look, you fucking leech. The rules are simple. No money, no pop. Get yoursen a job and a wash and then come out.*

Turkish leans back in assessment. Fry is almost asleep, waiting for the next drink.

Wilk is now looking around the table. *I know you think I'm being a cunt, Turk, but he has to be told like this. It's the only way of getting through.*

Shaun of the Dead now sits as if on trial, silently waiting the verdict. There is something artificial about his shame.

*I know, Ron, but there are ways of telling a man.*

With the prospect of an ally, Shaun leaps in for the kill. No finesse or social graces whatsoever. *Will YOU borrow me a tenner, Turkish? I'll give it you back, promise.*

There is red in the face of Wilk. *Always the same fucking script, ya paraffin lamp.*

Turkish can sense that Shaun is seconds away from being backhanded off his stool, so he raises a gentle hand in the space between them, lets out two short coughs, calming things down, taking control with a Gandhi-like power. Wilko restrains from violence by taking himself to the bar.

*Shaun, I will not borrow you ten pounds, nor will I LEND you ten pounds. I am on a very short budget myself, and I simply cannot afford to fund you every time we go out. Like you, I am also out of employment, but I regulate my outgoings so that I can allow myself to live as I choose. I suggest you do the same.*

Turkish was the only one whose first language wasn't English. Yet he spoke it far better than the rest of us.

Wilk returns with a tray of drinks.

Shaun now writhing in a pit of doom, watching as Wilk hands out the pints.

He knows exactly what he's doing. Taking a long satisfying tug on the John Smith's. Leaning back, stroking the glassful of ale as if it were a breast. Sucking up the fumes. Drinking with eyes closed as if it were a spiritual moment, before punctuating the whole sequence with *aaaaaaaaaaaaaahh.*

The stool holds a slumped Shaun. The pint-less space before him is an abyss.

*You know what the best part of a day session is, lads?* Wilko sings at the top of his voice. *When you've had a couple of jars and the beer is kicking in. There's a good team out. High spirits. Fanny to look at, money in your pocket and a whole night ahead of you. Can't beat that feeling! Imagine having to go home now. Half-cut but nowhere to go. The drink wearing off in the middle of the afternoon. On your own, hungover, while the rest of the lads are out having a laugh. Fucking tragic, it is. I wouldn't wish that on any cunt.*

He swings his big mug right into Shaun's face and laughs into it.

If Shaun had the physical capability, Wilk would be a dead man. The hate in his eyes is quite disturbing.

Something in Wilk's masterful taunt rings hard in my ear. And then I remember. I glance up at the clock hanging on the back wall.

I have to be at work in less than two hours.

### Sparky & Sidekick

The door claps violently, making us all jump. Two more figures enter The Joseph Else. One short, one large. Short leads, large trails. Short is Sparky. Baseball cap. Swinging gold chain. Burberry tracksuit hanging off his puny frame. Eyes manic, dancing above a toothless smile.

*Yeeez ma bredders.*

Sidekick heads straight to the bar.

Starting with Fry, Sparky works clockwise around the table, big-fisting everyone. His energy infectious, his smile never-ending. With each bump of the fist, there is *yes, bless, seen.* Yet when he gets to Li'l Ron Wilk, there is nothing. Just a little white fist hovering over the big man's bulbous gut.

Sparky nods, thrusting his arm forward. *Touch, man.*

*Don't start that spook shit with me.*

Turkish sighs and looks away, hurt.

Fry seems utterly oblivious to everything.

*Naahhh.* Sparky leaps back, his hand snapping away as if he's been zapped by an electric fence.

With his deep frog-like voice and well-timed rapid hand gestures, Sparky goes into theatrics.

*Man, dat iz raaacist! Ya know me woz raaiised by Rasta fam.*

Wilk takes a swallow and then goes back to neutral.

*I don't care if you was adopted by Bob Marley and the Wailers. You either shake my hand like an Englishman or fuck off.*

With an opportunity to redeem his position, Shaun sides with Wilk.

*Your dad int a Rasta anyway. I've seen your dad. Saw you both down Hyson Green, remember? The cunt's whiter than me.*

Sparky takes off his cap and gives his crown a scratch.

*First off, yeah, ma dad int a cunt. And secondly, yeah, he ain't white. Do you know why he ain't white? Cah he iz black. B L A C K.*

Sparky puts his fist out for Fry to give a second touch, which he reluctantly gives. Fry's face blank with confusion.

Shaun has been without a drink for a good twenty minutes. With a need to stay in the game, he is determined to keep the conversation rolling.

*No, Spark, you definitely introduced him as your dad.*

Sparky stands back and sizes him up.

*Man, will you close dat bin-eatin', cardboard-livin', soap-dodgin' mout of yours up bled. Man 'ere iz chattin' shit. Me was raised by Rasta, man.*

Sidekick comes back from the bar. Hands Sparky a pint before standing behind him like a docile bodyguard. Eyes glazed and bloodshot.

*All right, Stu, how are things?* greets Turkish.

*Sound, man, sound.*

The atmosphere takes on an awkward edge for a few moments, mostly due to Wilk having his party crashed. The attention no longer fully on him.

Sparky and Sidekick stand next to each other like a double act.

Sparky looks mischievous, like he is about to pull something off. Suddenly he flinches hard, feigning shock, looking up at his mate. *What. You still 'ere, ya six-foot pile of shit?*

*Well, I would be,* Sidekick counters. *Paying for your ale all day, ya scrawny cunt.*

Sparky goes onto his tiptoes and starts mimicking his speech. *Waa, waa, waa, waa. Who taught ya to speak, man, Forrest Gump?*

Table breaks with laughter, even Fry, even Wilk.

With his audience won over, Sparky goes in for the kill.

*And will you get outta ma face … wid dat nasty lickle bret.*

Sparky cranes right back, face in disgust.

*What ya on about my breath?*

*You, man … you is in possession of some lee-tal bret.*

*What you on about, my breath le-ful?*

*Waa, waa, waa, waa. What, is ya hearin' as fucked up as ya talkin'? I said ya bret is lee-tal. Man, never 'as I experienced a bret like dat. Dat iz some hazardous bret. Dat bret is danger. Dat bret is crucial.*

Wilk is now broken. Fry is back to life. Shaun is drunk again on the sober spirits of pure laughter.

Sparky goes on. *'Ere wot, bredrins, my man 'as et onion. My man 'as et skunk. My man 'as bin chewin' on roooottting corpse.*

Sidekick takes two short breaths into the cup of his hand.

*Dat's it, bled, inspect dat bret for yourself.*

Sidekick's face is nonplussed. *Well, I don't know what you're on about.*

*Waa, waa, waa, waa. Man, dat is cah you is impervious. My man 'ere is even immune to 'is own bret.*

My sides burn. I'm in physical pain. I can't see straight. I need a piss.

*Yeah, well …* Sidekick ventures. *You've got no teeth.*

Sparky stretches his rubber body and jumps on the spot, firing back.

*Listen, yeah … I would prefer da teet dan da bret. 'Ere wot I would prefer no teet whatsoever dan be in ownership of dat nasty lickle bret.*

Sidekick is beaten. In the end, all he can do is accept it as Sparky waves the crowd in closer.

*Please, bredrins. Come sample dis bret. Take a personal whiff. Smell for yourselves. See dat dis is no conspiracy.*

*Fuck off,* bawls Wilk, his thumb arrowed at Shaun. *I've had to put up with this smelly cunt for the last three days.*

Sparky waves everyone in. *Come, come.*

Being seated the nearest, I have to go first.

Sidekick steps over me; dull eyes, faint smile.

*Sample dat shit and tell me I'm lyin'.*

Sidekick opens up and lets it out. It hits me. I feel it all over my face. My hair blows back. It's bad. I almost expect to see a colour, green or a murky yellow. My reaction alone sends the table into further hysteria.

*See, dat's what I'm talkin' about.* Sparky drops his arm with a click of the fingers.

Sidekick goes around the group. Bar Wilk, everyone has a blast. Fry takes some persuading. Turkish nearly throws up, and Shaun shows no reaction at all. Others who have joined the table are unfortunate in getting roped in.

Sidekick seems strangely flattered by all this, his role. He glows.

Like any master, Sparky finds a way to close it out.

*And ya know what else, peeps ... ya won't believe dis ... but my man 'az even 'ad mints ... imagine da bret ... befoooore da mints.*

I'm wiping tears and trying to catch my breath when a text comes in.


### Marianne

*Thank you for standing me up, Robin.*

*I went out and bought a new dress for our dinner date, so thank you for standing me up. And thank you for cleaning all the sick from around my bathroom. And thank you for drinking my champagne. It was a gift by the way. And thank you for leaving the empty bottle on the worktop. Like rubbing my nose in it.*

*But, most of all, thank you for snooping when I asked you not to.*

*What a good human being you turned out to be.*

I go to reply but something distracts me.

Shaun of the Dead banging into my arm, spilling my pint.

*Shit, Robin, sorry, Robin*, he says in one sentence.

*S'all right, mate*, I say.

From nowhere, I have my wallet out, taking one of the twenties.

I hand it to Shaun and he seems breathless, pale, almost like he's about to faint.

*Get 'em in, Shaun, and keep the change.*

I wink and give his face a light double-slap.

*Keep the change, but I hardly know ya*, he mumbles in the smallest of voices.

I say nothing.

Tears in his eyes, *I'll pay you back, I promise.*

*Maybe you will, maybe you won't*, I say coolly.

Shaun is gone, up to the bar with a new strength in his stride. His swagger is back.

### Irish Blood

The table has been laughing non-stop for the last half-hour. Other people in the pub steal needy glances in our direction. They want in. They want to be a part of it all. Sparky has become God. He has owned us. There hasn't been room for anything else other than this laughter, this joy. Any pain anyone has is long gone. It's moments like this that all the hangovers become worth it. All the lost jobs and broken relationships start to mean something. The trade-off seems to balance itself out. The universe has equilibrium. Where in the world do you get this kind of realness, this timeless degenerate beauty? Characters and more characters, ever-flowing. This is *the life*. The life of pub. And all the sacrifices we make to have this life, *earn* this life, become worth it in these rare, raw moments. It's here I decide, one hundred per cent, *fuck work*. I'm ringing in sick. I mean, what choice do I have? I'm Irish after all. It's in the blood. It's a part of my genetic makeup, my heritage. It's out of my hands, really, not my fault. I'm not responsible for the way I was made. I think of all the great Irishmen of the past, storytellers and poets and rebels of my long linage, and let myself off for the way I live. It makes sense, a complete justification for my marvellous misdeeds. I watch Shaun of the Dead at the bar now; smiling, happy, totally blissed-out at the prospect of more hours. I have bought him some time. I have kept him in the game.

*I* did that. I gave this to him.

A gift. Camaraderie after all.

He'd do the same for me, I'm sure.

Wouldn't he?

### Romance

Another empty glass and I'm back at the bar. Back with Bang-Tidy Gothy-Thing.

*I'm done with the pints*, I say. *Time for top shelf.*

Her big dark eyes look at me funny.

*Why you talking different?* she says.

*What?*

*What's with the accent?*

*Eh?*

*Sound Irish or something?*

*Oh, to be sure.*

I point at something top shelf and off she goes.

When she returns, I slap a note on the bar. *I'm ringing in sick*, I announce.

*O-kay.*

*Yeah, there's no way I can go into work with that lot down there.*

We both look across the pub.

*What do you mean?* she says.

*Well, I know it may not look much from where you're standing, but honestly, it's fuckin' electric down there.*

Her black lips make me think of liquorice. She smiles a touch.

*And what do you do?* she says.

*What do you mean?*

*Your job, ringing in sick?*

*Oh, I just sit with a retard and watch telly.*

She pulls a face. *You mean, like care work?*

*Support work.*

*And you're ringing in sick?*

*Yup.*

*Time you start?*

*In about an hour.*

She pulls another face and goes to serve someone else.

I catch her wrist and she looks at my hand on her wrist, and then at my face.

*Hey, you wanna grab a drink sometime?*

*A drink?*

*Yeah, like a date.*

*What?*

*Look, I know we're probably into, like, way different things. You into all that goth stuff and probably spend most of your time at Rock City and whatnot. And me, well, I'm out here, aren't I? But, look, I've always had this massive thing for you. You're stupidly hot and I've never really gone out with a girl like you before.*

*A girl like me?*

*Yeah, but I think we could make it work. Opposites attract and all that. So, what do you say?*

She parts her mouth and looks up at me, then at the other customer waiting to be served. Back at me.

*You know what?*

*Yeah.*

*Think I'm gonna pass.*

She walks away fast ... and hard.

*Oh, okay,* I say. *That's cool.*

## Ringing in Sick

Stood at the top of the stairs, by the disabled toilets. There's a phone in my hand and a voice in my ear. I think it could be Nadine but I'm not sure.

*Robin?*

*This Nadine?*

I think she says *Yes.*

*Listen, Nadine, I'm not coming into work. I'm ringing in sick.*

*Oh, you're taking the fucking piss.*

*Sorry.*

*Robin, please come in.*

*Can't.*

*Why?*

*Just can't.*

*Robin, you're a fucking selfish prick. Means I'll have to stay, and my boyfriend's supposed to be taking me out tonight. Bought a new dress and booked a table and everything.*

An image of Marianne.

*Sorry.*

*You always fucking do this.*

*I can't help it.*

*Yes, you fucking can, though.*

*Trust me. I can't.*

*Why?*

*I'm Irish.*

*What?*

*Nothing.*

I feel her rage in the silence.

*So what is it this time?* she says.

I pause, think, trying to conjure something up.

I can hear the magic behind me. Wilk threatening someone. Sparky's deep Jamaican tones, exploding the room into more wild laugher.

Then I see Fry's forlorn figure move past the slot machine.

*My grandma,* I say.

I almost say it in Fry's Yorkshire: *grandmaaa.*

*What?*

*My grandma,* I say mournfully. *She ... she's just passed away.*

*Robin.*

*Yeah.*

*Oh, Robin, I'm so sorry.*

Fuck. What am I saying, what have I said?

Shaun of the Dead suddenly appears from nowhere, planting a kiss on my cheek before disappearing into the disabled toilets.

*Robin.*

*Yeah?*

A full Niagara sound of Shaun pissing next to me.

*Robin, I'm so sorry. I didn't realise.*

*It's okay, Nadine.*

*Where you now?*

I pull the phone away from me and pull a face.

Shaun flushes, leaves the disabled, another kiss on my cheek.

*Just at the wake,* I say.

*Oh.*

I feel how confused she is.

*Yeah, yeah.* I sense I'm about to fuck this up.

*Robin.*

*Yeah, we Irish, we kind of have two wakes. One the day they die and one after the funeral.*

*I see.*

*This is the first one.*

*First one?*

*First wake, yeah.*

*Listen, Robin, don't worry about tonight. I'll explain to Lez.*

*Thanks, Nadine. You a star.*

*Listen, you take as long as you need.*

Sparky is now standing on a table with the crowd around him. Gothy-Thing tries to get him down.

*Yeah, I'm supposed to be on tomorrow*, I say, keeping the grief in my voice.

*Hey, if you need me to cover, I will.*

*Might be best, think I'll be feeling a bit rough tomorrow.*

*Hey, I get that.*

*Thanks, Nadine.*

*No problem.*

*Sorry I spoilt your night.*

*Robin, it's fine. There's more important things in life.*

*Nadine.*

*Yeah.*

*I owe you.*

There's a strong silence between us.

*You just take care, and send my condolences to your family.*

*Thanks, Nadine.*

She goes to hang up but I catch her one last time. Something else has just popped into my head. *Oh and, Nadine?*

*Yeah.*

*Do you know if we've been paid yet?*

Another bewildered pause.

*Er, oh. Yeah. We have. Wages went in about an hour ago.*

I close my eyes and tense right up and sprint on the spot. Adrenalin ricocheting through my body, before slowly steadying myself. Back into character.

I can tell she's confused by this question but I no longer care.

Right now, I feel invincible, bulletproof.

Don't think I say anything else, just hang up. Hang up on Nadine.


## Back in the Game

I was never out of it.

*My round!* I yell at the top of my voice.

Shaun of the Dead swoops onto my shoulder like a parrot.

Wilk lands a love-punch, deadening my arm. *Good lad, Robin.*

Sparky up in my face. *Yeszz, bredders … now dat's what I'm talkin' 'bout.*

Sidekick by my side. *I'll give you a hand, Robin.*

Fry is nowhere to be seen.

It's a tray of double voddys and Red Bull. Gothy-Thing gets someone else to serve me. Fuck her. Fuck the mardy bitch. *Where I'm going, we don't need roads.* People moan that this isn't their drink but fuck them too, cos my brain doesn't come with a short-term memory, right now. I've bought about a dozen and I hand them out. The spares I just give to whoever is in the vicinity. Shaun has managed to take two drinks. Right now, I am in awe of how Shaun can work the room. A whole day on the lash with zero pence. I could learn a lot from him.

And at this rate, I might need it.


### D.H. Lawrence

I head to the toilet to piss out what I've just put in. Strip it all away and this is what life basically is. Circles and cycles. Eating, shitting, wanking. Waking then sleeping. *The Sopranos* ends; *Breaking Bad* begins. Easter followed by summer followed by Christmas. Seasons, years. A decade. I realise I have a bit of a stagger on. Gothy-Thing dead-eyes me as I pass, and I wonder if I said anything too bad when asking her out. I can read the future. Just as I'm passing the food part of the pub, a soft voice calls out.

*You strike me as somewhat of a literary man.*

I turn and see fuck all there and wonder if I'm finally losing it.

*Women in Love.*

*What*? I say.

*Sons and Lovers. The Rainbow.*

Before me is this red-bearded little fuck wearing a flat cap.

*I won't mention his most famous one cos it all becomes a bit too obvious, doesn't it?*

He's drinking an orange juice and staring at a framed picture on the wall.

*He's from round here, you know?*

*Who*? I say.

*Old D.H.*

I stand next to him and we look at the picture.

*Look at his wormy eyes.*

*Yeah, he's from Eastwood, innit?* I say.

*That's right.*

*Not read owt of his, have you?*

*Here and there.*

I notice a book in his jacket pocket, green cover poking out the top.

*That one of his?* I say.

*I beg your pardon.*

*The book you have there.*

*Oh no, not quite.*

*What is it then?*

He's still staring at D.H. and the little prick is starting to freak me out a bit.

*It's your life story.*

*What?*

*I'm only on page 80, but I'll let you know how it ends.*

I'm completely captivated by this cryptic cunt, but the piss-feeling is so heavy right now I'm about to burst.

*Can I get you a drink, mate?*

*Sure.*

*Sound.*

*But I don't drink, not alcohol anyway. I quit thirteen years ago.*

*Thirteen, unlucky for some.*

*Unlucky for you.*

*What?*

*I'll have another orange juice.*

*I'll just go and piss it out first.*

He nods slowly, still not taking his eyes off D.H.

I vault the stairs and collapse in the toilets and piss into the urinal for what seems like five full minutes. My head is in bits with the weirdo. *Your life story.* What the fuck.

Bladder better, lighter.

I head back upstairs.

Once there, I see – he is gone.

I line up and look into Lawrence. He was right; he does have wormy eyes. Knowing little eyes. Beady and brilliant. It strikes me how much the guy looks like him. Small, bearded. For a moment, I really believe I could be losing my fucking head.

*Shaun, you see a guy wearing a hat walk past?*

*What?*

Not a reliable witness, so I move on to Turkish.

*Turk, you see a guy wearing a flat cap, standing near the food bit? You see him leave?*

Turkish does his trademark raising of an eyebrow. *No, Robin. I have seen no such man.*

I must look worried.

*You look worried*, Turk says.

*Nah.*

*Are you all right?*

*Yeah.*

*You sure?*

*Yeah, look, have you seen Fry?*

*Now that is a man I have seen. He's sat outside in the Market Square. I think he's had enough of this crowd. I think it's starting to get to his head.*


## Dead Grandma

He's sat right there in the Square, almost asleep. Fry does this a lot. He's always either just waking up or nodding off. Stooped in slumber.

I notice the massive England flag festooned across the council house, ready for St George's next week.

I call out his name and it stuns him awake.

A string of drool glistens in the sun.

He wipes it with the back of his hand and looks at me. *Our kid.*

*Sup?*

*Nowt.*

*Why you leave?*

*Can't be doing with that lot in there.*

*Tell me about it.*

*Fuck off, Robin, you love it.*

I look around at people in the Square. Everyone seems so normal. People waiting and meeting at the lions, the left one.

*I can't be doing with that Wilk*, Fry says.

*I know.*

*I can take a joke, Robin, but I've got my limits. Do you know what he said?*

*What?*

*He said … what have wogs and dogs got in common? They're both either vicious or stupid. I mean, fucking hell, Robin ... I'm sat RIGHT NEXT TO HIM.*

I watch Gothy-Thing finish her shift. A gothy guy meets her at the door. They kiss and then head towards Friar Lane.

*Then that Sparky. He's funny, yeah. But he keeps tryna big-fist me every five minutes, like I'm his long-lost brother. He's fucking whiter than you!*

I laugh.

*It's not funny, Robin. This race thing starts to get tiring after a while.*

The early-evening air sobers me up a bit.

*Thought you had work anyway?*

*Rang in sick.*

*Shouldn't be doing that, bruv. You're lucky to have a job.*

*Told 'em my grandma had died, ha!*

Fry throws his head up and looks at me hard. *What?*

*Needs must, man.*

Fry is on his feet. *You're fucked up.*

*What?*

*I'd do anything to have my grandma back, and here's you ... lying about her death.*

I close an eye.

*I mean, technically, I'm not lying. Just thrown her forward a decade.*

*You're sick.*

*Oh, c'mon.*

I put my arms out as Fry stands and turns away from me.

*I'm off, me.*

He heads off across the Square.

I shout up after him, *Fry ... Fry, it's just because you're getting your emotions back ... remember what your drug worker said ... it's because you're getting your emotions back.*

People look at me like I'm a nut.

My eyes follow him up towards the lighted neon of the Hard Rock Cafe.

I can almost see myself standing under it.

Sober. Smart. Going on a date.

Twenty-four hours ago.

I was a completely different man.

# Windmill City

I re-enter to the sound of smashing glass. A female scream cuts through the air. The whole pub has gone up. Wilk is windmilling some youth into the fruit machine. An old man ducks and weaves around the violence, trying to retrieve his winnings before blood is splashed all over the shop. Other fists fly. Two women plunge nails into each other's hair. Another bottle breaks on the wall.

Sparky gains a foot in height, standing on one of the high stools.

He produces the impressive effect of looking really tasty yet not actually doing anything. His bony hand flexed into a gun-shaped fist, scurrying all over the place like a fleshless rodent. *Watch, watch, watch.*

He strategically moves behind Sidekick. With an extra body as a barrier, he amps it up. *Manz gettin shot up. I'm danger. I'm danger. Boom, boom, boom.*

Wilk knocks one man out and moves on to the next.

The only one who seems to be prospering from all this is Shaun of the Dead. He swoops down on unattended drinks. Settles on them like a vulture. Drains the life out of them before flying off to find another. Someone left without a dance partner eyeballs me, and I am pulled into it. I throw out a combo but am too fucked for it to have any real impact. My feathery fists just crumble against a bald head. Luckily, Security break it up before he has a chance to hit me back. A siren whines in the way distance, slowly growing in volume. Some dipshits stay and argue, waiting to get arrested. While most of us move on, staggering along the tramlines.

Shaun vomits in a bin.

Wilk spits out a mouthful of blood.

Turkish the pacifist probably left before it kicked off.

Sidekick holds a bloodied hand, slight scuff above his eye. Sparky is untouched.

From nowhere, Vic has appeared, looking up for CCTV, before sliding a knuckleduster into his back pocket.

# The Roebuck Inn

The other Wetherspoons, the good one.

Two women are stood at the bar next to me.

*What was that fight all about?*
*Wilk just started on this black guy for no reason.*

I take a red wine and go into my own world. More conversations go on all around me, swimming through my ears.

*Sparky, man, ya did fuck all, just waved your rubber gun around for half an hour.*
*Waa, waa, waa. Man, all you 'ad to do was open dem jaws and unleash da bret and da rumble would have been over time ago.*

*Where's Turkish?*
*Where's Fry?*
*Pussies.*

*See Sidekick scrap? Fuckin' hell.*
*Can't beat Wilk, though. Must have took out five of the cunts.*
*King of the Windmill!*

*See Robin, skipping about like a ballerina.*
*Yeah, but he's a lover, not a fighter.*
*I heard he's fucking a tranny.*
*What?*
*Yeah, my cousin Michelle told me.*

*Did you know Wilk has a daughter? Honestly, mate. Spitting image.*
*Poor bitch, mug like that.*
*Fuck's sake, don't let him hear ya.*

*I reckon I'd tek him on the cobbles.*
*Wilk, mate, ya a tasty cunt, yeah. But Carl Froch is a professional boxer.*
*Different on the car park, though, innit?*
*What, ya get knocked out on the tarmac instead of the canvas.*

*Hahahaha.*

*Is that Vic?*
*All right then, keep your voice down.*
*He's had people buried, y'know?*
*Did he know the Gunnies?*
*Shut up, you silly cunt.*

*Hey, I only shag homeless birds. So much easier to get them to stay the night. And after you fuck 'em, you can drop 'em off anywhere.*
*Hahahahaha.*

This is England. *Load of shit. Fuck all on Gary Oldman's* Nil by Mouth.
*Not seen it, mate.*
*Fuckin' masterpiece.*

*Who's Forest got at the weekend?*

*We getting the fuckin' ching in then or what?*

*Robin, Robin.*

I hear my name.
   *Robin.*
   It's Shaun of the Dead.
   *I know this might be tekkin' piss. But ya couldn't throw us another score, could ya? Just till Monday. Get my giro Monday.*
   Absent-mindedly, I open my wallet and pluck out another note and hand it to him. He moves in for another kiss on the cheek. A bone-crushing squeeze to go with it. I'm sure he'd stink if I wasn't so pissed.
   Once he's gone, Wilk is at me. *Soft cunt, you are. Think you're getting that back? It's twats like you who keep him going. Enough people say NO and he might have to get a job.*

## Red Wine

is my drink. Normally at the end of the night when no one really gives a fuck. Can't be drinking this out with the lads. I drink it on my own. I drink it in my flat. It's a different kind of drunk to all the other types of drunk. It's *in*. It's *down*. It's dreamy and drowsy. Insular. It lays me down. The feeling always makes me feel like I'm someone else and somewhere else. A poet crossing from Spain to Tangiers.

It makes me deliciously maudlin.

The lights blur and soften, like a Van Gogh.

I'm thinking about Marianne right now, how thoughtless and cruel I've been.

I take out my phone to text her, but another girl has magically appeared in my lap.

## Quaz

Her breasts scream under my chin. Her face is something else. Beady, bewitching eyes. Tiny black dots of starey madness. Double neck. A troop of blackheads crowd her forehead. But mostly it's the teeth. Big, frightening, discoloured tegs.

*Fuck you drinking red wine for? You posh or summat?*

*Mind your business.*

*You gonna fuck me or what?*

I look at the tits. Then at the face. The two negotiate with each other in my head.

Tits: *C'mon, these are incredible.*

Face: *So is this.*

Tits: *You can't keep your eyes off them.*

Face: *Yes, you can.*

Tits: *It's worth the sacrifice.*

Face: *I'm not so sure.*

Tits: *Sneak me out now and the lads won't see.*

Face: *Too late. They're all looking at us, look …*

I look. All of them spread across the bar.

Wilk, Vic, Shaun, Sidekick and Sparky. All five faces leering in a line.

*Pulled yasen a right little stunner there, Robin?*

*Got some top bollocks on it, though, hasn't it.*

*He's used to bollocks, though, from what I've heard.*

*Don't do it, Robin. Ya a good-lookin' lad. Tap that and your rep is fucked.*

*Yes, man … my man is checkin' Quasimodo. Don't let her get the hump wiv ya, bredrin.*

Sparky turns to the fit barmaid. *'Ere wot don't ring da bell for last orders; uvverwise, Quaz will tink she's back in Paris.*

*Hahahahahahahaha.*

Sparky has material for another set and the crowd gathers around him.

*What they on about?* Quaz says.

*Nowt.* I pour the wine down my throat. *Just being pricks.*

*Oh.*

*Wanna get out of here?*

She nods. Her face is hideous. Her eyes are sad.

I follow her tits out of the pub to an almighty cheer, tables banging, glasses clinking.

A laughter so mad and dizzying my head spins away from itself.


## Chambers

*Can't we just go to a hotel?*

*One more drink.*

I can barely put one foot in front of another, yet the drive to drink is still unstoppable. We're sat in the corner. For a moment, I forget where we are.

*There's a hotel just next door*, Quaz says pleadingly.

I don't even answer her. Just focus on not being sick. I stare at the empty chair next to me and concentrate on holding my stomach down.

At the end of the bar I see that weird fuck from earlier. Red beard, flat cap. He's drinking orange juice again. That green book in his hand.

*Story of my life.*

Who the fuck reads in the middle of a boozer?

I try to get up and ask him about it but fall back down, splashing into Quaz's tits.

*You all right, babe?*
I slur.
*Don't drink any more.*
When I look up again, he is gone, just like the last time.
*I'm fucking up.*
Quaz looks quizzical, concerned.
*Let's just go to that hotel next door.*
*Okay*, I nod. *Okay.*

### Britannia Hotel

They turn us away. They won't let us in. I try to contest it but I can barely string a sentence together. Quaz tries saying that I just have food poisoning. I think she even refers to me as her husband. In the end, I kick off and Security has to escort us off the premises. I collapse through the big revolving door and it takes us around twice. For the first time, I hear Quaz's laughter, and I note how sweet it is.

*Can't we go back to yours?*
*Can't we go back to yours?* I counter.
*I live with someone ... but ... but we're not together.*
I note the chill in the air.
*Maybe if you make yourself sick, you'll sober up.*
I look at her face.
*No hotel will let us in like this.*
*Yeah, they will*, I say. *C'mon.*

### Bentinck Hotel

Vic is squatting by a tramp in the doorway.
When he sees us, he laughs madly. *Robin, Quaz.*
*Why's he keep calling me that?*
This day seems to have no end.
The tramp is dark-skinned and foreign. He has a guitar.
Appears like they've been talking for hours. It is the dead of night.
Everywhere is closed.
*Drinks at mine! Put ya hand out for a cab. You too, Desperado.*

Homeless man can't believe his luck. Grabs his guitar and stands, dusting himself down.

*Look 'ere*, Vic says. *This is my fuckin' town. I live out in the country and I'm rich. Big fuckin' yard. Try robbing me, ya cunt, and I'll set the pit bulls on ya.*

Tramp and Vic pass a bottle of tequila back and forth.

*And we want a song on that fuckin' guitar an' all. Earn ya keep. Know any Justin Timberlake?*

A cab in the distance, but Quaz has already pulled me through the door of the Bentinck.

I can just about hear Vic screaming into the night air, *Where the fuck have they gone?*


### Nicotine Walls

and dust and damp patches everywhere. On the carpet. On the bed. The dark waters of the canal move beneath us. I move the crusty curtain and gaze through the grimy windows to see Vic and Guitar Tramp disappear into a cab, pulling away from the kerb, heading to the countryside of Tollerton and his gangster mini-mansion.

When I turn around, I see a naked Quaz, crawling towards me on all fours like the girl in the music video.


### 'Cradle of Love' by Billy Idol

Only the effect is a little different from that goddess who plagued my pubescent dreams as an eleven-year-old. Her face snarls. Her teeth and tits scrape across the carpet. I'm stood before her, swaying like a fatalised character in *Mortal Kombat*. Her hands reach my shoes, before she starts to slowly climb up my legs, unbuckling and unbuttoning me as she goes. Her eyes look scary and her tegs even more so. There is evident disappointment as she pulls me out.

I hear her mind go, *Is that it?*

*I'm a grower, not a shower,* I say.

*Grow then!* I hear her mind say.

She works it hard but it doesn't get hard. Nowhere near.

I could be deep-throated by a chicken.

Feel like I'm inside a cheese grater. Or, with this size, a pencil sharpener.

Never knew that fellatio could be an ordeal, a punishment.

Then from nowhere it comes.

It comes.

Comes not cums.

From the pit of my stomach right through my chest, throat, mouth.

A torrent of vomit.

Proper projectile.

The sudden retching seems to sound through the entire hotel.

It lands on her naked back, slaps against her skin, thuds against her bones.

Cubes of carrot slalom down her spine.

Then there is silence.

Then she looks up at me.

And I am so shocked that she doesn't seem shocked by this, at all.

# Day Three
# The Fool

'They took the water out of the pool because I'm not a good swimmer. I'm bad at sports and, at school, nobody wanted me on their team.'

From the motion picture *The Swimmer* – starring Burt Lancaster

# Her Name is Actually Rox

not Quaz.

She rolls over and looks at me. *Well, that was fun.*
 Daylight smashes through the window and burns my eyes.
 *Can you close the curtains?* I say.
 She skips off the bed and pulls them across the sun.
 *I've been up an hour,* she says.
 *Good for you.*
 *The coffee's shit.*
 The room warps and wraps around me.
 *Want one?*
 *What?*
 *A shit coffee.*
 *Isn't there a bottle or anything about?*
 *Eh?*
 *We bring owt back last night, any booze?*
 *Nah,* she says, looking around. *And I don't think they have a mini fridge.*
 She pounces on the bed and grabs my head.
 *Fuck's sake.*
 Her face is worse in the morning; lopsided and grotesque.
 *My name is actually Rox, by the way.*
 *Oh.*
 *Your mates kept calling me Quaz, but that's just rude.*
 There's a bald patch on her head that I hadn't noticed last night.
 *I'm no oil painting, but that's okay. I've had a lifetime to get used to it.*
 There's an immediate fearlessness in her eye that catches me off guard.
 *I must be really ugly. You couldn't get hard last night.*
 She pulls at the duvet and snorts.
 *Nah. Amount I drank last night. Result would have been the same if I was gang-raped by Girls Aloud.*
 Rox tilts her head. *You're rude, like your mates.*
 She gets back into bed and takes off her top. Her huge tits drop out.
 *Wanna give it another go?*
 *Sure.*

If I look at her blackheads, I'll be sick. If her discoloured teeth come near me, I'll be sick. If I catch a whiff of her Jack 'n' Danny, I'll be sick. Instead, I keep it close and tight. Roll on top and slide it in. Despite all this, the grip is hot and good. Makes my eyes water and clears the hangover for a few moments.

So good that I feel myself about to blow from the off.

*You fixed?*

*No, you?*

*Can't wear 'em.*

*Why is it always the woman's——*

*All right.*

*So what we gonna do?*

*I'll have to pull out.*

*Hope your timing's good.*

*It will be if you shut the fuck up talking.*

*You're rude.*

The sex is short, stiff and awkward, like two Down syndrome kids dancing with each other at a disco.

Pull out and shoot across her gargantuan breasts.

I'd say.

I'd say that, between us, that is the only sexy scene we nail.

We lay, holding.

*This is nice*, she says.

Her stumpy finger traces a pattern across my chest.

*You're completely hairless, like a girl.*

*All right then*, I snap.

I think about giving her an insult back, only there's too many to choose from.

*Hey, no need to be sensitive, Mister. I'm not saying it's a bad thing. I actually quite like it.*

Rox's beady eyes trace the long length of my thin torso.

I cover up.

*I need a drink*, I moan.

*Want me to get you a glass of water?*

*I mean a drink-drink.*

*Oh.*

*Yeah.*

*It's probably not even ten.*

*I know.*

*Are you an alcoholic?*
*Yeah.*
*Do you drink every morning?*
*Nope.*
*Do you drink every day?*
*No.*
*How can you be an alcoholic then?*
*Just am.*
*Binge drinker?*
*A problem is a problem.*
*Oh.*
*And the biggest problem right now is not having one.*

She squints and twitches. *Want me to go out and get you something, bring it back?*

A surprising twist of sweetness turns in my chest, and I find myself holding her colourless head of hair.

*Nah, s'all right.*

*Think I'm still pissed*, she says.

We lay for a bit. The sounds of mid-morning Nottingham on the other side of the window. Sound of someone sweeping the street soothes me, and we may even drop off for another hour. When we wake, we shower. Hygiene. I remember I skipped a day yesterday. It's weird cos we wash each other off naturally. Completely non-sexual, like a married couple of fifty years. My hideous body and her hideous body. Me: thin, white and full of ribs. Feline and effeminate. Contrasting to her misshapen mass of rolls, craters and saggy flesh. Neither of us abashed, just getting on with the practicalities of sharing our ablutions. Wash my back and I'll wash yours.

### 'Don't You (Forget About Me)' by Simple Minds

plays in the breakfast club bar. It's like a school canteen minus the kids. We give our room number before helping ourselves to more shit coffee and orange juice. In the fridge, I hallucinate on a can of Stella Artois.

*Shit. I thought that was a Nelson.*

*Nelson?*

*Nelson Mandela.*

*Eh?*

*Nelson Mandela … Stella.*

*I don't—*

*Stella Artois.*

*Fuck, you really have got it bad.*

*I've got it under control*, I lightly muse. *Gonna retire at age thirty.*

*How old are you now?*

*Twenty-seven, you?*

*Thirty-two.*

*Oh.*

*Toy boy*, she smiles.

I feel like that comment should freak me out but it doesn't. The energy between us is calm, almost serene. Being around her makes my hangover seem not as bad. She doesn't bug me. She doesn't *go on*. I get no needy or gamey vibes from her at all. Like she can take me or leave me. Everyone in the breakfast bar notices her appearance. A middle-aged man peers over his newspaper. Slight smirk coming from a small group of squaddies. A stunning black girl, curiously by herself, gazes over and considers us. Rox seems used to this. She is grounded and non-reactionary, accepting. Something grows within me. Something really admires the way she carries herself. There's an inner power I've not seen in a human for a long time.

I'm not really hungry, but letting a free full English slide seems foolish. I remember not eating a morsel yesterday, not after the scraps of food I picked at Marianne's.

With the threat of another day on the pop, I really should get a foundation of snap in.

Lining the stomach, they call it.

## Vic

His name flashes violently in the centre of my phone. No more than three forkfuls into the brekky and here he is. I think about letting it pass, but fear has me punching the green button and taking the call.

*Just got to take this*, I say to Rox, who is now tunnel-vision on the egg, bacon, sausage, tomato, mushroom, beans and toast.

I note the dry mouth and the shortness of breath. Adrenalin, which is starting to work its way around my body.

*Vic, good mornin'.*

Already there is chaos in the phone.

*What the fuck. Can you tell me why I've got a bloke locked in my conservatory?*

*What?*

*I've got a baseball bat in my hand and the cunt's head's gettin' caved in if you don't tell me who he is in the next ten seconds.*

*How the fuck do I know who he is?*

Rox's eyes dart up from the plate for a second.

*So you saying he's a burglar?*

I hear commotion in the background, a voice and then a scream. Something smash.

*Vic, slow down. I don't know what you're talking about.*

He tries to slow down, gather himself.

*I've just come downstairs in my boxers, cracked a can and popped some toast when I hear this knocking on my conservatory window ... and there's some fucking hobo stuck on the glass! What the fuck? I'm about to bat the cunt, but he's screaming in a foreign voice, 'No, sir, no, sir, my friend, you bring me here. You no remember?' NoIdontfuckinremember.*

Suddenly I remember, and laugh out loud.

*Robin, what ya laughing at? The cunt's got some guitar ... trying to defend himself.*

I hear frightened Spanish. Vic talking to him now. *All right then, cunt, shut the fuck up. I'm getting to the bottom of it now.*

Rox is on to the last of her sausage. I watch her shove and scrape it through her teeth. I get a flashback of last night and wince.

*For some reason, he remembers you. 'Ask your friend,' he says. 'Robin and ugly girl, call them, call them.' So, cunt ... that's what I'm doing.*

I start to eat while I talk.

*Put the bat down, Vic.*

*So he's right?*

*Poor fucker.*

I feel Vic calm, and then shout at his guest. *All right, duck, calm down.*

*Can you at least give him the thumbs-up or summat?* I say. *Bet he's 'bout had a heart attack.*

*Cunt, aren't I?* Vic is laughing now. *Honestly, Robin, I don't remember a fucking thing. Not a Scooby. What the fuck am I doing bringing a tramp back to my pad?*

*Think he's a busker, slight difference.*

Vic talks more to him.

Then back to me.

*Thought I was having a stroke when I first woke up this morning. The whole side of my face.*

Rox is now looking fully at me, intrigued.

*Where are you anyway?*

*Stayed at that hotel, didn't I?*

*Which one?*

*Bentinck.*

*Fucking hell, mate, no one stays there. What the fuck. Even the rats bring a packed lunch. What ya stay there for?*

I scratch the back of my head awkwardly. *With that girl, aren't I? Which one?*

Rox still looking hard at me.

Vic's memory must have suddenly kicked back in. *Not that fucking Quaz!*

I try to muffle the phone but it's too late. She looks away.

I feel shit. I feel bad. I really need a fucking drink by now.

*Right, we back on it then?* Vic screams.

Excitement pricks my guts, popping the hangover.

I hear Vic unlock his conservatory and slide the door. *All right, Pedro, calm down. Make yourself at home, lad.*

My breakfast is tepid by now. I've only managed about half of it.

Vic goes business mode.

*Right, you, Bentinck, yeah, by the canal. See you at Waterfront in an hour.*

The line goes dead. Another day is born.


## Goodbye, Rox

I feel bad she blatantly heard it. No punctuation needed. Rox carries on regardless. I start to move in preparation now. Slowing things down, closing things off. Starting to separate myself from this night, this morning, *her*. That coolness, that coldness, this awkwardness. Mouth moving but the brain elsewhere. She watches me closely. She sits still as I move around in my chair. Looking out the window, looking at the clock.

*So*, I say with a breath, *So. I've just got to nip out for a moment.*
I stand up, fake a stretch and yawn.
*Don't do that.*
*What?*
*Don't spoil it, Robin*, she says calmly.
*What? I'm just—*
*I've been with enough bang-and-bailers to know how it goes. Don't be one of them. You're better than that.*
She sits up, flicks her hair.
*Overall, we've had a nice time. Okay-ish night, shit shag but beautiful morning.*
The *beautiful* she says with real feeling. *Don't spoil that.*
I fight back the urge to defend/excuse/make light of the *shit shag*, but instead I hear her out.
*If you've got to go, go. But don't sneak. Don't slink off. Look me in the eye and say goodbye. I'd like that. I'd respect that.*
I go to make another excuse, but something in Rox's courage gives me courage.
I unbutton my top button and face her. Take her hand.
I go to agree with her that it was a *beautiful morning*. The kip, the shower, the snap. Only I feel it's all *a bit much* and can't handle that, so instead I simply say, *Goodbye, Rox.*
*Goodbye, Robin.*
I go to leave but the strength in her grip keeps me there.
*Be kind to yourself, Robin.*
*Will do*, I nod.
I go to leave again but still she keeps me.
*No*, she says. *I really mean it. Be kind to yourself.*
This time, I don't say anything; just look at her. Her beady eyes hold me. Like she can see right into me, and I don't like it. My whole naked history is exposed to her. I nod and break away. I would have kissed her on the cheek, had a hug, maybe even given her my digits for a future friendship, but right now I've got to get away from here, from her.


## Downstairs

Not far from home. Just a dozen or so steps away until I'm back in my beloved Bridewell Bar. Bentinck Bar. No way I can face Vic dry, so a fresh pint of cider is before me in no time. Fuck, do I need this. There's an unusual sadness in the centre of my chest and I don't know why. I look at the ceiling where Quaz is sitting above me. Why has this freak got to me so much? She was right; it was a *shit shag*, but that's got fuck all to do with me. See the state of it. I mean, is she punching or what? And then she's got the nerve to tell me to be *kind to myself.*

I neck the cider, turning thoughts over. Knowing that I have probably missed the opportunity to make a good friend. A special friend. I look at my life and think of all the good and special friends that there are: none.

Phone. Two texts.

Vic: *On way cunt.*

Cassidy: *Where are you bro?*

Cider has always been my perfect hair of the dog. First one of the day. Watery, fruity, light and easy to get down. By the second one, I'm totally cured. Totally *back on it.* In fact, it tops me up quicker than I expect, and I'm pretty much pissed again.

### Fracas

Orange digital at the bus stop: 10.37.

Way earlier than I thought.

Just then, the belting blare of a car horn. Followed by a window down and an angry red cunt screaming at a cyclist. I've seen this guy before. Think he used to live in my flats. Stocky, squat. Red face, red hair. Always pumped up. Always screaming at his kids.

*Get in ya fuckin' lane.*

Cyclist calmly swings off his bike, takes his earphones out. *What say?*

Red Man spits and snarls. His head about to explode.

His mouth moving, mad; only I can't hear because of a passing bus. Cyclist is going nowhere. He makes gestures with his hand diplomatically. I'm kind of concerned for him cos Red Man looks like a tasty cunt. Yet at the same time the cider is swimming in my skull and I want to see some street entertainment. Despite the rage of Red, Cycle takes a step forward, slowly pulling off his gloves.

Now Red undoes his seatbelt, making a big physical display of it. Cycle shrugs. *Yeah and what?*

Red is out and now the fracas pulls in attention from the entire street.

Cycle is smaller, shorter and slighter. They square off but not quite. A lot of flinching and shuddering and circling. Not one punch is thrown.

At last, Red gets back in his car. This retreat fills Cycle with full confidence. He takes his hat off and moves right up to the vehicle, which quickly speeds away.

Cycle now stalks the street as Red gets stuck at a red light. His delivery is easy, street-smooth and pleasurable to hear. *Fix up 'n' flex. Get back in your whip and MOVE, fam. Yo, ya seen how dis man make a big show of himself to the peoples, yet he don't fully roll like me cah I'll do this fo real, man ... dat's it, fam. You drive on like da lickle pussyole dat you is ... embarrassin' yourself in front of da peoples-dem ... come find me, fam ... come find me ... ya seen my face, fam ... ya know my name. Come find me and I'll be waiting all day every day.*

He rolls off between the red lights, standing sideways on his bike, two feet on one pedal, not giving a fuck.

## Waterfront

First thing I see is a guitar. Word WATERWAYS in white-bricked font on the front of an old building, high in the hangover sky. Its reflection breaking in the dank green waters of the canal. I walk the two bridges. Stone one and the iron one.

Vic and his busker.

The pair have obviously healed since being parted by a conservatory door.

Busker in a more settled space since his night of incarceration, and the near-miss of being baseball-batted to death by one of Nottingham's leading figures in the underworld. The two sit in the dubious sun, working on a pair of Kronenbourg 1664s.

*Robin.*

*Lads.*

*Where's the stunner?*

*Did a runner on me, didn't she?*

Busker is smiling.

Vic looks absolutely wrecked. Gonna take a few more hairs of the dog to get him right again.

*Didn't fuck it, did ya?*

*Don't be silly. It was my sister.*

Best way to play this one, I calculate. Be vague and nonsensical. Give away nothing.

*Fuck me, Robin. Seen some states in my time, but she was next level.*

For some reason, I feel mad, and with a primal need to protect her.

Say something like: *She has more goodness in her little toe than you have in your whole soul, you barren vacuum of degenerate scum.*

*Yeah, I know, man*, I say. *Laugh, though, innit?*

*Is it? Fuckin' disgrace is what I'd say.*

The busker's name is Miguel, and Vic insists on calling him *San*. He's from Bilbao and he's travelling around Europe through the summer. Busking, hitching, chilling and meeting people. Sleeps where he drops. His story sounds fascinating, but the minute we get on to anything of depth and culture, Vic bulldozes right through it. He can't stand to have the conversation out of his control, so as soon as we touch on Hemingway, Goya or the Guggenheim, he has to come in and spoil it all.

*All right, cunts, I'm here to have a booze and a nobble. Not listen to your boring bollocks all day.*


## City of Rebels

A walk through the bus station and the back end of Broad Marsh.

Bliss. This morning-after-alcohol feeling has me hovering through the crowds.

*I know what you mean*, San says. *It's fluid, effortless. It's an ego suppressor after all. In the night, alcohol can be too much, too forced and crazy. But in the morning, the residual effects have transcendental qualities.*

*You're right, San. You're so right. It's like there's this silent, secret interconnectedness with everything and now I see it.*

Vic has stormed off. *Can't wait to get into Wethers with some normal people. You two are weird as fuck.*

San and I float through the people.

*You're so free, man,* I say. *No job. No responsibilities. No one to answer to. What a fucking life. I need to learn an instrument.*

*Get a djembe drum,* he says. *Learn it in a month.*

*I'm gonna do that,* I say. *I'm really gonna do that.*

As we get to the other side of the shopping centre, San suddenly stops.

*I've just had a premonition,* he says, putting his guitar down. *A vision.*

I wait for his next words.

*One day, I see a big green sign here,* he says.

People are looking at him.

*The sign says ... City of Rebels.*


## The Joseph Else

I enter Wethers to the roar of applause.

*Fuckin' Robin!*

All eyes are on me and I don't know why. Like it's my birthday or they've mistaken me for a famous person.

Wilk leads the onslaught. *State you pulled last night.*

Shaun of the Dead: *John Merrick's twin sister.*

More lads I barely know jump in:

*Little fucking stunner.*

*The fucking tegs on it.*

*Scary, mate.*

*Halloween come early.*

San Miguel can't get his head around why they are treating this like a celebration, bedding an ugly girl. He's confused; a culture shock. Wilk, who barely acknowledged me yesterday, aims his attention at me like a loaded gun. Arm around my neck, feeling the full force through his breezeblock shoulder.

*Get this man a pint. Any man who tackles that deserves a free day on the piss.*

The ethereal journey from Waterfront has now been crushed like a dirty fag into an ashtray.

*Fuckin' good-lookin' lad like you an' all.*

Wilk holds my eye contact for a moment too long and I feel myself squirm. His lips are extra red.

Vic is scratching his head.

*Cunt seems a bit loved-up to me*, he says. *Way he's been staring off in the distance, you'd think he'd had a night with Natalie Wood.*

*Natalie Wood? Showing ya age there, Vic*, someone says. *This is 2008, not fifty-eight.*

*Wood?* Someone else cuts in. *Looked more like Ronnie than Natalie.*

Another wave of laugher ripples through the pub.

The circus settles and we take a seat at three large tables that have been joined together on our arrival. Shaun seems more relaxed today, perched on a high stool like lord of the manor. He's obviously rumbled coin from somewhere. The day ahead has been taken care of. There's a new cockiness to the man.

When I come back from the bar, he's pulled the people in via some banter with Wilk.

*You're a tasty cunt, Wilk, I'll give you that. But Carl Froch is a world champion-to-be.*

I seem to remember hearing this conversation last night. A strange sense of déjà vu sets in. I know the next sentence from Wilk before he says it.

*Different in the car park though, innit?*

And the next line too.

*What, ya get knocked out on the tarmac instead of in the ring?*

I'm a bit freaked out by this and again wonder if I'm starting to lose my mind.

I look at San Miguel and this humour is totally lost on him. He hasn't got a clue what's going on.

The tables erupt and for the first time I see Wilk totally stripped of power. He cowers for a moment. He looks like a boy. Shaun of the Dead howls at the ceiling like a demented wolf. He becomes king, revelling in the secret pleasure others feel at watching Wilk crumble. As the laughter fades, an eerie silence sweeps through the tables. Wilk readjusts, takes in a quick intake of breath. His eyebrows lift and I see it before it happens, a malevolent psychic flash. It glides in from the left. A swift perfect backhand. It slams into Shaun's face. Half-slap, half-punch. The sound stuns the room. Shaun's face, blank with shock. His eyes moisten with the filling of tears. The pain becomes vicarious. We all feel the hot sting rinse through his cheek. Humiliation drains through him from top to bottom. All eyes hit the floor. Apart from Vic, who glares at Wilk with judicial venom. Who in turn takes his pint casually, as if nothing's happened.

Someone breaks the silence and the atmosphere resumes.

Shaun doesn't speak for twenty minutes. When he does, it is something forced.

*What d'ya reckon to the Brian Clough statue they're putting up over the road in November?*

Someone answers, barely.


## Mid-Afternoon

2pm, then 3pm. For some reason, I can't get pissed and I don't mind this. I'm sober. Or, I should say, I *feel* sober. Sober*ish*. I'm shimmering, simmering. I'm in the slow cooker, bubbling away. I am full of booze. Made up of it. It's in my blood. It *is* my blood. Pumping through my system like a normal bodily function. It is not a foreign agent but *a part* of me. I could drink another five pints and be the same. Ten, fifteen maybe. To do any damage now, I would have to hit top shelf. That is the only way to get to the next level. But I don't want this, not yet. I am deathly relaxed. Other than the bar or taking a piss, I could sit here until the end of time.

Everything is … just fine.

At some point, a crackhead comes in selling shoplifted steaks.

Gothy-thing isn't working today, which is good cos I get to give my libido a rest.

I watch Vic perform the conservatory anecdote for the fifth time today. He corners a small audience, playing out his animated baseball-bat theatrics, before switching roles to the hands-up/scared-to-death part of his destitute guest, who by now has done one. Backdoored it.

San Miguel has done a runner.

San Miguel has done a runner without saying goodbye.

San Miguel has done a runner without saying goodbye, and I feel a little sad about that.

Yet at the same time his mysterious departure is kind of fitting, kind of perfect.

I absorb the poetry of it.

Like most people in here, Vic is a master storyteller. With each telling, the tale gets more exaggerated. By now, it's like watching a violent version of Charades.

## Heather

Text:

*Ayup Robin. How's things x*

The name *Heather* confuses me at first but then I remember. Girl I used to knock off about a year ago. Bit of a drinking partner. Bit boyish but not a bad-looking gal. Bit of a laugh until she started a relationship with this boz-eyed cunt twice her age.

She's obviously sent the prick packing and is back in the game.

I get a little jolt of excitement with the prospect of Round 2.

*Heather, my girl, what's going on? Xx*

A swallow of beer and another text back.

*Not much u got a job yet? x*

Odd question, I think.

*You know me, girl. Come day, go day ☺ x*

*Yea I no you well x*

Something strange about this. Heather was normally high energy. Can't remember this retarded illiteracy either.

*So when we back on it then, my girl? X*

*Back on wot?*

I'm starting to get a bit bored now and wonder where Heather's personality has gone.

*The booze. A drink. A night out or an afternoon session. x*

*Hm not sure after last time.*

*Last time? x*

*I meen were we in a relatiosnip or wot?*

Penny. Dropped.
    This ain't Heather.
    This is the boyfriend.
    This is Boz.

I type out a text, calling him out.
    Thumb about to press *Send*, but then a better idea comes to mind.

I catch myself smiling in the reflection of the window.
    I note the pub noise fade out around me.

*Heather. Although not officially together, you were my love.*
*You were my love and I have never made it so sweetly, as I did with you. x*

My guts do somersaults as I read it back. *Send.*

There's a massive pause this time. I imagine the boz-eyed cunt. Staring at the phone. Staring into space. His whole world come undone.

At last, something back.

*Think ya gods gif don't ya. Well im glad I ended it. Wiv a better man now.*

I tap the phone against my pint. My mind alive with possibilities. I can see that the cunt isn't too bright and probably not possessing much in the way of emotional regulation. My calculation is that I probably have one more message before he loses it and the curtain falls.
    Gotta make this one count.

*Heather, My Girl, I miss it all. Everything that was US. The loving friendship wrapped in lust. The way you looked, smelled, touched and tasted. The way we talked all day and fucked all night. The way we transcended conventional relationship and made our own rules, reached our own heights. Orgasm definitely brought us enlightenment. Unreal how in tune our bodies were. Cosmic. Never had it before and not had it since. Most of all, I loved how patient you were in accepting my size. Contrary to what most men think, and wish for, carrying This Thing around is actually a curse, not a gift. Totally impractical and most girls ran a mile. But, Heather, you didn't. You accepted me. I know it wasn't easy. But week by week, inch by inch, we got closer and closer to our heaven. I'll never forget that night we came together, the multiple orgasms you experienced, again and again. Baby, I thought you were never gonna stop.*

*But aside from our mind-blowing masterpiece of a sex life, it was the little things I adored. The million parts of you.*

*That mole on your hip. Your sexy toe rings. That cute little scar to the left of your flower. Almost a signature. It's these imperfections that made you perfect, in my eyes.*

*Anyway, Heather, I know you're in a relationship now. Like you say … he ain't much to look at and not the sharpest tool in the box … but … he is safe, simple, a sure bet. And that's what your life needs right now. I'm always here to fall back on. And as much as I don't agree with infidelity as a whole … for you, I make an exception. If the sex does get any worse … then please give me a call.*

*I can't bear the thought of you being unloved.*

*PS And don't worry about our last time.*
*I mean yes technically it was after you made it official with him.*
*But we all have our careless little crossovers.*
*It's today that counts babe.*

*Yours, forever, Big Daddy Robin*

Yep.
This is victory.
This is a landslide.
Maybe even slightly overkill. But,

fuck it.

Send.

## Lucy Kite

I watch her while I wait for the reply. Soundlessly delivering the weather on one of the overhang TVs. She's going for the sexy look today.

Figure trim and clipped in a sharp red dress.

Hair up, revealing her wineglass neck.

She looks taller than normal.

Must be heels.

## Boz

He doesn't even do texts anymore. Just straight to calling.

Of course, I let him hang.

Before sending a text a few minutes later.

*Heather, so happy to hear you calling.*

*Just heading into a business meeting baby.*

*Some big bucks coming our way if it goes alright.*

*All the better for taking you out for a long-awaited, much-deserved feast, my sweet.*

Reply:

*I fucking knew it!!!!!! Fuckin knew she was cheating and and fucking new it ws YOU. Ohhh your dead m8. Fuckin Dead. Ded meet. You have crossed the wrong man this time you sick skinny man. I'll find out where you live mateOh. Boy. Its gonna hurt!!!!!!!!*

He tries to call but again I let it slide.

I'm laughing so much it hurts, putting a score in Shaun's hand, waving him to the bar for a refill. I read his words over again and decide that the boy uses too many of them to be truly dangerous.

Most dangerous people I know are as silent as sharks.

You don't hear them coming.

Vic wanders over and plonks himself opposite.

He's proper pissed now. Just staring into his half-empty glass.
I motion at Shaun to get him one in too.

My next text:

*What? Heather? Are you okay? Who is this?*

After I send, a feeling of horror drops into my stomach. *Heather.* I
have completely forgotten about her in all this. *Fuck.* Regret moves
across my scalp like slow hot headache. What have I done?

*U no very well who this is?*

*Boz?*

*Cheers, Shaun*, I say as he puts down the pints. I have to wave my
fingers for him to give me change, which he does with a sigh. His
face is still red. An imprint of a hand from Wilk's slap.
*What's tickled you*? he says, leaning over, trying to spy at my
phone.
*Oh, just a joke between old friends.*

Text:

*What did you fuckin call me?*

*Boz. That fucked-up eye in your head.*
*Boz is the pet name Heather and I call you.*

*Robin, stop!* I tell myself. *Why are you doing this to Heather?*
*What has she ever done to you?*
*The danger you could be putting her in.*
Hear this all the time in the news. Humiliated men who *flip.*
Stick a knife in or strangle to death.

*Shes fuckin dead anall. You both are.*

*Come get me then.*

*When?*

110

*Now.*

*Where?*

*Wethers on the Square. You sound like you've had a few jars yourself, lad. Let's have a few drinks and sort this out like men.*

*Oh ther will be no talking mate.*

Noticed his messages are getting shorter and to the point. A certain finality to them, which is putting me on edge.

*Fine.*

*On my way.*

I'm smiling but not smiling. Smiling on the outside but shitting it on the in.

What if I've totally underestimated my enemy?

What if he's more than just a retarded-looking man in his forties?

What if I've just poked the beast of a full-blown psycho without realising it, without thinking about it? I've been drinking near constant now for almost forty-eight hours, and Reason is something I'm no longer in possession of.

*On my way.*

Why would he say that if he didn't mean it? Those three short words fill me with dread, doom. *On my way.* My first instinct is to backdoor it. Do a runner. Yet the thought of being on the streets alone isn't a good one, either. Funny how this little episode has magnified my true masculinity. On the outside, I'm slapdash and showman, caveman, cavalier. Yet on the inside, I'm a baby deer trapped in barbed wire. I look at the clock, at the passing of time, slowly becoming a quivering mess.

Maybe I need more drink.

Maybe I need

## Top Shelf

I get a double JD cos that's what Wilk's drinking and slide in next to him. He seems a little confused that I've singled him out and bought him a drink and am sitting next to him. Quite up close, actually. I don't say anything but fold myself into a ball. It's like I have my head on his shoulder or in his lap. I try not to appear too needy cos he might fuck me off. There's a strong squad of lads out by now, and I'm feeling safe and insulated. I look at the door, waiting for the oncoming figure of Boz, but nothing arrives. Often, I look down at these that I drink with. Inferior beings who have never read a book between them. Builders. Bouncers. Butchers. Men in the market, the factory and the warehouse. Broom pushers, shit shovellers. Illegal men, dangerous men. Tough lads. Tasty cunts. Last men, first men. Men on the top shelf. These are the men we hide behind when shit hits the fan. These are the men on the front line when the wolves come knocking at the door.

I look at the door and I look at the door.

Then my phone rings.

I see a name on the screen and shit myself as it says Boz. And then I'm confused cos I don't remember putting his name in my phone but then realise it doesn't say Boz at all but

## Boss

I let that call slide too and a text comes shortly after.

*If you don't call me back in the next 5 minutes, Robin, your job is gone. 100%. End of.*

More fucking panic now, and this is turning out to be an afternoon of Hell. There is a spiral and this man Robin Goode is at the centre of it. I'm also aware I'm starting to refer to myself in the third person. A thing I often do when I'm trying to separate myself from myself. When I am trying to avoid myself. Save myself.

Before he thinks about it too much, he is calling his boss back.

The long ring on the phone is agony, but at last Leslie, my boss, is on the other end.

Her deep voice, much deeper than mine, is poured into my tab like gravel.

*Robin, you little prick, where are ya?*

*Pub.*

*Which one?*

For some insane reason, I think Boss and Boz could be connected somehow and paranoia grabs me.

*Just—*

*Listen, you need to get to work.*

*When?*

*NOW.*

*No.*

*Don't fucking NO me, you selfish arsehole. And don't start with your dead grandma bullshit, either. How many fucking grandmas have you got? Two died last month and now a third! Right fucked Nadine's night up last night, you did. Put the poor gal on a 24hr shift! Well, you're not doing that to me. I'm leaving here in twenty minutes and YOU are taking me off. Otherwise, Robin, you're gone. End of.*

I find myself agreeing. I find myself saying *yes*.

*Now …* Boss's voice calms down, measuring herself slowly. *All you've got is Darren. The others have all gone home. Get him fed. Put him bed. And then the rest of the night is yours. Stick the telly on. Cuppa tea. Camp bed out and then you can sleep it off. You don't even have to do any cleaning. I can't be much fairer than that, can I?*

No, she can't. And I find myself saying, *Thank you, Lez.*

*You coming?*

*Yes.*

*You on your way?*

*I'm on my way.*

*You won't let me down?*

*I won't let you down.*

A contractual silence fills the phone.

*I'll see you in twenty.*

*You'll see me in ten*, she says. *Catch a cab. I'll pay the fare when you get here.*

She kills the call.

# Options

I consider them. I consider them carefully. Carefully but quickly as I start downing my pint.

Shaun of the Dead is staring me out, confused.

Options.

Option One:

Don't go in. Let her down. Lose my job.

Positives: I get to stay out. But stay out for what? A psycho hunting me down for the rest of the night. Not really a positive, is it?

Negatives: No job. No money. No rent. No booze. No dates. No fanny. Just the hassle of jobseekers. My social life/drinking life reduced to being with Fry 24/7. Raising coin. Begging. Shoplifting. Methadone mornings. White Storm afternoons. Days of daytime TV. *Loose Women. This Morning. Jeremy Kyle.*

Fry constantly going on. The same things again and again.

*Swear on my grandmaaaa'sss grave.*

*Gettin' my emorrrrtions back.*

Going on about Cheryl Cole every ten minutes.

*She's beeew-ifff-fulll, bruv.*

*It's been proven … she's got the best eeeeyyyyeeeessss.*

*If I could just get a girl like that, I'd be happy. I'd chhaaaaaannnnggeee.*

Option Two:

Go in. Don't let her down. Keep my job.

Positives: Avoid a psycho hunting me down for the rest of the night. Stop spending. Stop fucking up my liver and my brain. Go into a warm, safe house with cupboards full of food. Big comfy sofa, big TV. Drink tea and have a laugh with Darren. Tell him my war stories over the last few days and listen to his. Jump off now while I'm not feeling too bad. Climb slowly back on that wagon while I'm just about *compos mentis.* Take advantage of Boss's Tough Love, her firm but fair position. Help her to help me in this final act of leniency, bordering on charity.

*She's even paying for your taxi, for fuck's sake.*

Negatives: There are none.

I down the rest of my pint.

*In a bit, Shaun.*

*Where you goin'?* he says.

*Work.*

He looks at me as if I'm speaking Ukrainian.

Then panic lights up in his eyes as I straighten my clothes and head towards the door.

*Couldn't throw us one more ten, could ya, Robin?*

Still heading towards the door.

I don't look back.

### Taxi

It pulls off, leaving the city. Victoria flats in eyeline, moving up Mansfield Road.

Text. Boz.

*Here. Where are you?*

Reply:

*I was bored of waiting.*

*Oh u chicken shit pussy!*

*It's you who was faggot.*

*I'm in town mate. Where U?*

*On my way to Heather.*

Again, I am sickened at how I keep using Heather like this, yet for some reason I can't stop.

*U goin hers?*

*She coming mine. And trust me, she will be cumin.*

*Am gonna cut that fucking dick off.*

*Make sure you donate it to Twycross Zoo when you do.*

*Fuckin coward mate. Got ur cards proper marked now.*
*Shown yasen for the pussy you are.*

*Still in Wethers?*

*Yup.*

*Why don't you ask around for me?*
*They all know me in there.*

Now I'm using more people. Hoping he'll rouse a Wilk or a Vic into action.

Getting people to fight my battles.

All this assuming they'd care enough to bother. Who knows? The right words from Boz about fucking another man's Mrs (which I haven't even done), and those lot could quite easily be turned against me.

Now the paranoia is full blown.

As I sober up, a self-hating shame starts to malignantly grow in the centre of my psyche.

*Fuck you on about???*

No more texts now. I put my phone away as the taxi takes the suburban side streets of Sherwood to my place of work. A black and white detached house behind a moss-stoned wall.

My boss stood at the door.

She resembles a bouncer rather than the manager of a care home.

Doesn't say anything, just fixes me with a strong, knowing contact of the eye before barging past me, disappearing into the cab I have just stepped out from.

### Darren

He sits there smiling with his eyes. The sober, silent surroundings freak me out a bit. Darren in his usual chair, in the corner, under the lamp. Lit up like he's on a game show. Through his goatee, a schoolboy smirk is stitched into his face that says, *I know what you've been up to.*

*All right, Daz?*

*Puck off, ya cunt.*

Darren swears constantly. In the middle of words sometimes. It's a part of his brain injury. A Tourette's kind of a deal. His Fs are Ps.

*Wanna pucking tea, my man?*

His voice sounds like a blocked-up Hoover.

*Go on then, Daz.*

*Pucking sober ya up, ya pucking cunt.*

He wobbles onto his feet. Adidas tracksuit hanging off his crippled frame. It always amazes me how Daz doesn't break his neck every five minutes. His lopsided gait. One side of his body fucked. One dead leg dragged by the other and a gimpy arm hooked at his chest like a wing.

*You a pucking alcoholic, you are.*

*Takes one to know one.*

*Too pucking right.*

Darren was, is. That's how he got his brain injury. His mate got a massive pay-off for being hit by a bus outside Broad Marsh bus station. Darren tried the same. He actually *chose* to jump in front of a bus. Only he got left for dead instead. A metal plate in his skull. There were a dozen or so witnesses who watched his insane stunt. Got not a penny.

Now he just thinks it's funny. Slapping his plate. Doing his comical DJ dance. Grabbing his balls. *Pucking puck 'em all.*

He brings me a cup of tea. Pendulum of saliva swinging over it as he hobbles and puts it in my hand.

I tell him the story of the last few days. Full boyish bravado.

He sits before me, delighted. Struggling to breathe as I pull in all the details.

Fat bird. Tranny bird. Getting knocked out. Champagne. Scrap in Wethers. Ugly bird. Vic and the tramp. Boz.

In return, he tells me about all his birds and scraps and wild nights.

Being a runner for the Gunnies. Prison sentences. Time he was a pimp in Amsterdam.

After I've made him some snap and all the soaps are done, I feel the hangover in the post. I say hangover, but at this point it's more than that. It's *withdrawal.* One night is a hangover; a few nights and days and we go into withdrawal.

*Pucking struggling, ma man?*

I'm now supine on the sofa. Horrible things happening in my head.

*Not bad, Daz, not bad*, I manage.

*Hey,* he says. *Can we put it on?*

Oh. Fuck. Not sure I can handle this.

Darren is obsessed with a film. He watches it three times a week at least. More if he could get away with it. He mimics the dialogue word for word. His impressions are funny, but I'm not sure I can handle it tonight. Not now. Not like this.

*All right,* I say. *All right but keep it down. My head's fucking killing me.*

His screw-face smooths out with a big beamer.

*Pucking love you, ma man. My pucking favourite pucking staff. Hands down.*

*You say that to all the cunts.*

Gives me a wink and then hobbles over to the DVD collection.

Pulls out a case, opens it and shoves in the disc.

TV lights up. Menu page of Coney Island. Red writing across the screen.


### 'The Warriors'

1979 cult classic by Walter Hill. Darren goes mad. Starts dancing and shouting out the iconic line:

*Warriors, come out to plaaayyyy.*

Drool pooling his Adidas tracksuit.

*Fuck's sake, Daz, I said keep it down.*

*Pucking sorry, my man.*

My head in bits. Glance at my phone, which is still lighting up with texts and calls from Boz.

*Wan' another pucking tea, my man, before it pucking starts.*

*I'll make it,* I say, standing up and shaking myself off.

I head to the kettle and make the tea, turning a thought over.

*I shouldn't come down like this. It's dangerous. To my physical health and my mental health. I need a soft landing, a gradual touch-down. The old pyramid system of doing it one level at a time.*

*The Warriors* is in full swing by the time I put Darren's tea in his hand. His arm inked in self-made tattoos. *NFFC. UB40. Denise. Tracey.* A prison number proudly displayed, Auschwitz-style. *Cut here* circled around his wrist in a succession of dots.

He's up and down on his feet, running off lines of dialogue from the film.

*Cyrus ... he's the one and only ... what's up, goin' faggot ... can you dig it, suckers!*

I stand watching him, fidgety, making up my mind on something.

*Hey, Daz.*

*Pucking what?*

*Fancy a crafty can while we watch this?*

His mouth drops open then smiles. Nodding his head.

*Too pucking right. You a pucking legend.*

*Just one, though,* I say.

He nods, clearly excited. Putting his eyes back on the screen.

As always, the withdrawal gets put on ice by just the mere thought alone. The brain is amazing like that.

*Oh and, Daz.*

He looks up.

*Anyone rings, tell 'em I'm just on the shitter.*

He nods and then I'm out the door, into the night air. Polish off-licence is only minutes away, bottom of the road. A four-pack of Tennent's Super. Rocket fuel, tramp juice. Darren's favourite. All the time, I am bargaining with myself.

*Poor cunt. Stuck in here. Life as he knows it is over.*

*So what if I'm treating him to a little tipple while he watches his favourite film.*

*Doing a good deed,* I tell myself.

I enter the home to *The Warriors* line of:

*We're not gonna hide who we are just because some whore shakes her ass.*

Darren and I crack a can and toast it.

*To* The Warriors, I say.

*We are the pucking warriors, my man, puck 'em.*

## Pizza

I sling one in the oven. It's on the menu for tomorrow but fuck 'em. *Puck 'em.* The can is done in no time and my phone is back out, winding Boz up again.

*Been showing Heather your texts.*
*We've been having a right laugh.*

Instantly, he tries calling me.

*Can't talk now Boz. Kind of got my mouth full.*
*So has Heather.*
*Main course on table 69.*

*Urrrrr fuckin dead!*

Darren has paused the film just before those iconic lines.
*I'm going to my pucking room to get the pucking birthday present you pucking got me, my man.*
*And I'm going back to the shop to get two more of these cunts!* I say, shaking the second empty can.
Darren lifts his good arm and points at me.
*Pucking best friend I've ever pucking had, you are.*

## Birthday Present

When I get back, he is wearing it. The *Warriors* jacket I had shipped in from America. Cost a fucking bomb. Half my week's wages but well worth it to see the look on Darren's face.

The jacket, a burgundy leather waistcoat with *The Warriors* badge on the back: a skull with the scalp on fire, two eagle wings sprouting up either side.

We sink our third can and I'm well trolleyed again. I make a note to make it Darren's last cos his eyes are starting to go and he's struggling to stand. We link arms and get ready for those epic lines in the film, clinking our cans together in unison with the actor David Patrick Kelly.

Both of us, all three of us; Darren, Robin and Luther, leader of the Rogues:

*Warriors come out to pllllaaaaeeeeyyyy ... Warriors ...*

From somewhere outside of this mad bubble I hear a sparkle of laughter, feminine laughter; girls, women.

Through the living room window two honeys are peering over the wall. It's dark out there, but I can make out their hair, curves and lipstick mouths.

I jump up on the windowsill and shout through the top window.

*All right, gals. Fancy coming in for a party?*

*We're fifteen, ya fucking perverts.*


## The Snap

*Fifteen.* The word snaps me in two, shocks me into sobriety.

The world just got real and I rub my eyes to try and see their faces clearly. Up until now, they had just been a girly blur. An overwhelm of fear and shame. Hoping to God that this is just a wind-up by some twentysomethings.

Hoping to God. Yes, *God.*

I think, for the first time ever, I feel Him. *Him,* or something big and beyond.

The girls move out of the shadow and into the light. Their faces stark now, young behind make-up, swagger and defensive attitude. Their expressions change again, from anger to fear to pure horror.

Suddenly they become their true ages, maybe even younger.

*Oh my God,* one of them cries out.

I follow the direction of their eyes. To my left, I see Darren up at the window. It takes me a few seconds to realise that he's naked from the waist down. The tattered Adidas of his bottoms are around his ankles. His shrivelled two-incher pressed against the glass, squashed like a slug. Pale pink with a purple vein running through it.

His pubeless ball sack hanging like a rotting peach.

*Pucking sit on my pucking face, ya pucking bitch.*

*DARREN!* I yell so hard my voice cracks, and the girls run away, screaming.

*Darren, what the fuck have you done!*

His mad mongy face is in full hysteria, eyes rolling into the back of his head. His contorted mouth arrows into a triangle, more drool spilling down his top. Laughing so hard he starts to stumble back, first the good leg, then the bad one. He knocks his Tennent's Super and a giant pool soaks through into the carpet. On instinct, I try to pick it up, neglecting the fall of Darren, which is high from the windowsill. Smashing his head on the floor, an instant cut, blood washing with the alcohol, merging into a greenish-yellowing evil colour. My eyes are deceiving me surely. This isn't really happening. I run into the kitchen and grab a tea towel, two tea towels, three. Pressing them into Darren's wound, trying to stem the flow.

*This ain't happening this fuckin' ain't happening this really ain't happening just a dream just a nightmare.*

Phantom faces appear at the window, making me jump. Four of them. My attention on the two in the middle. Young white faces with lipstick and big eyes. It's the girls. Gawping in. It takes me a good five or ten seconds to see the two big blokes either side. Huge, mean men. Trying to work out what's happening.

Darren half-naked on the floor.

Cans of Tennent's Super littered all around the room.

End credits of *The Warriors* playing to the song *In the City.*

I stand up and go to explain. That he's just a poor brain-damaged man not responsible for his actions; only one of the girls points right at me, her finger shaking a bit.

*That's him ... he's the one ... he's the one, Dad ... he's the one who tried to get me in the house.*

Get her in the house?

The man's big beefy face growls into rage. He starts blasting the window so hard the glass rattles in its frame. Next, he tries the front door, and his mate unnervingly goes around the back.

I step over Darren, who has luckily stopped bleeding but is still unmoving. Both men are now checking all the windows and doors. I pick up the phone and think about the police. I punch in two 9s but can't bring myself to do the third.

*Fuck fuck fuck.*

I look at Darren and pray he'll start moving and that all this will go away.

Both men are now on the one door, the back one. And it's going through, no doubt. I see the wood warping and busting, bursting. It's only a matter of time. The hinges are about to give way. The handle about to pop.

I'm upstairs, then to the next flight where the fire exit is, right at the end of the corridor.

Still the noise downstairs. Like the whole building is being bulldozed.

I look through a side window to see neighbours coming out of houses.

As I hear the door come off, this one too opens. So high up with wind on my face.

On the flat roof but no way risking getting trapped on the stairwell.

Instead, there is a three-storey drop into next door's hedge.

I could quite easily break my leg here, neck, back.

But it can't be any worse than what them pair will do.

I see the word *maim*.

I hear them coming up the stairs now.

So I stand on the edge of the roof, lining up the darkness, trying to work out what is hedge and what is concrete. I feel my life spinning like a roulette wheel. A complete fifty-fifty.

City lights way in the distance.

A strobe of it moves across a patch of white night sky.

And I jump.


### And I Land

in one piece, I think, although I'm not sure. I'm upside down, looking at two tiny dot-faces. Way up in the high sky.

*What the fuck*, one of them says.

*Is he dead?*

*I'm going down there ... and if he is, then I'll kill him again.*

The faces disappear and so do I.

Up on my feet, hedge-hopping.

I'm twelve years old again, only with much more at stake.

It's a miracle that nothing's broken, or even hurting.

And it's then that I really believe I am living in a simulation, some video game.

The Holographic Universe.

None of this is real, and this notion suddenly gets rid of all fear. Moving from garden to garden, patio to patio. For an hour or more,

I venture through private backyard worlds like Burt Lancaster in *The Swimmer*.

## Mapperley Park

I enter the Beverly Hills of Nottingham at the stroke of midnight. I count a dozen gongs of the council house as I walk a silent tree-lined street. The drying sweat cools my skin. I am no longer thinking, just being. Just *experiencing*.

Wrapped in the comfort of shock.

So quiet – a gated community without the gate. Only reason to come here is if you live here. No shops. Nothing to do but look at *how the other half live*.

Giant houses with sprawling grounds. Old houses next to new ones.

Experimental postmodern architecture next to a row of Cotswoldian cottages.

An *Eyes Wide Shut* house on its own island.

A sleeping swimming pool shimmering through an apple orchard.

The roads roll and loop.

*Magdala. Tavistock. Lucknow. Cyprus.*

Trees and balconies and lighted windows.

Two tennis clubs, one at the bottom and one at the top. Mapperley Park climbs, rising away before dropping down into

## St Ann's

From one world into another, an opposite one. Separated only by the border of Woodborough Road. Down Robin Hood Chase. Into the urban maze of Stannz.

Stannzville.

*SV* graffitied into the underpass. *RESPECT 4 ST ANN'S.* A mural of multicoloured faces, speech-bubbled pleas floating from the mouths. *NO MORE VIOLENCE. LOVE. King Sim. More peace. Community Life 4 Eva. RIP – ALL THE FALLEN.*

Basketball courts and courtyards.

Clapboard church, like Louisiana gospel.

The yardz in the endz all tight and symmetrical, little iron bridgeways shared and connected to front doors.

Twenty minutes don't go by without the sound of a siren. Blue lights bouncing from the shadows, partially lighting up the path.

Memorial flowers left at spots in the road. *Danielle Beccan, Brendon Lawrence.*

Bandanas tied to posts, red Blood to the blue Crip of the Meadows.

White Man after dark.

At Corporation Oaks, I get the perfect side shot of my city's skyline, a stencil into the backdrop of the deepening night.

By the time I hit the centre, I am drained of all adrenalin and alcohol.

My feet are on their last legs and I know I need somewhere to drop, somewhere to crash, somewhere to sleep awhile.

## Maid Marian Way Roundabout

hums with a steady flow of traffic orbiting it. Even at this hour. I crawl into the centre and collapse. A dome of trees and bush surrounds me like a cave. I lay on my back. An ant runs over a leaf. The insect fills up the whole of the moon, which seems to get smaller and smaller as my eyes close.

## Moon

is gone when I wake. So is the noise. A dark breeze slips over my face and for a minute I think I'm naked. I roll over to see another body next to me.

*Marianne. Rox. Fry. Darren.*

I don't know where I am. I hear a car and flinch. The body stirs and sits up.

*All right, mate,* it says. *Normally have this island to mesen.*

*Where am I?*

*Like that, is it? Been there, pal.*

I look around and remember it all.

I nod at the green bottle between his legs.

*Give us a blast.*

125

He looks at it, worried.

*Yeah, all right, but don't go mad. Shops are shut now and it's got to last.*

*Time is it?*

*About three.*

I wipe the top and put it to my lips.

*Steady,* he says, his eyes never leaving the bottle.

I hand it back.

*I've got to get out of here.*

I get up and fight my way through the trees.

His voice follows me.

*Don't mention it, mate. Nice one. Keep in touch.*

The city is left for dead.

## Eclipse

Old pool hall on the outskirts of town. High windows a dark green. I climb the stairs to the left of the building. A deep bass reverberates under my feet. Big black bouncer wearing wraparound sunglasses. A white one who looks like he wants to rip my face off. I hand over money and they open a door. Faceless figures move slowly within. A sharp chemical taste in the air. This is the back end of the night. This is where they all end up. The people who can't bear to go home. The people who will take it to the very end.

Until the sun comes up. The comedown of birdsong.

An eerie Prodigy remix pulses through the large room. Most are monged-out in the chill-out corner, partitioned by translucent drapes. The sniffing is out in the open; keys and thumbnails. Nobody does lines anymore. A dozen or so are on the dance floor. The initial high long gone, people now just hanging on, trying to get it back, blasting out serotonin that their brains just don't have anymore. An orange bodybuilder dancing like a chicken, eyes shot and glaring, gurning. A skeletal woman in her sixties, all sinew and veins, just in her underwear. Every thirty seconds she screams out, but nobody seems to care. Two men in suits sitting in the corner, watching everything. There are people of all ages and races. The most common denominator is danger. Everyone looks proper

126

dangerous. Capable of real violence, in one way or another. This is a place of criminality. It is off-grid, illegal. Barely any booze left behind the bar. Just bottles of lukewarm Desperados. Just liquid to wash the pills down with. To stay numb.

Doesn't take me long to find myself in the arms of a girl. For once, I wasn't looking for it, but it found me. *She* found me. A small, squat, solid thing with a frighteningly familiar face. She puts something at my nose and I blast it. Burns the brain, and an instant rush. *Fuck, yeah.* Our tongues lash in each other's mouths, yet it doesn't feel sexual at all. A foul-tasting, aggressive exchange. Ashtray, acrid drip. Bit of blood.

We dance around each other and she hits me again with the drug. Doesn't feel like coke but then whatever. Hits me two or three times in the space of an hour. She's holding my hand and putting her arm around me, pulling me, yanking me. She's fucking strong, brutish and rough. Like she could really give me a good go if she put her mind to it. I really know her face but I don't know where from. A harsh wide face, pinkish and piggy. Her hair a dirty blonde.

*Gotta find my friend. Come with me.*

I'm now gripped by this drug and will follow her anywhere.

She's spitting and spluttering in my ear and I can't make her out. Something like:

*She's a good catholic girl and this is her first night.*

*Who?* I say.

*Luna.*

*Who?*

*You're gonna want to fuck her.*

*What?*

*Everyone has all night but she's mine. No one's fucking her unless I say.*

*What? Who?*

*LUNA.*

She points at a little dark girl leaning back on the podium, a flat brown stomach, belly stud winking through the dark. A guy is around her, but Piggy fucks him off as soon as we reach her.

*Do one*, she snaps at him.

Piggy in my ear again: *It's her first night. Her first night on gear. I'm looking after her. Good little catholic girl.*

# Luna

Her face drops when she sees me. Think she recognises me before I her.

*You bastard*, she says with a strung-out smile. Like she wants to hate me but can't with all the virginal narcotics running through her system.

*Luna, what the fuck are you doing in this place?*

I can't compute the two. *Her* being *here* and for a moment I have it down for some hallucination. Her attractiveness, her beauty, was bad enough wearing a waitress outfit, carrying dishes in her family's restaurant, but now in the full-blown, night-out, hair-down attire I'm almost knocked off my feet.

*You smashed all our windows, you bastard. My dad's gonna have you killed.*

*What? No.*

*Kimberly, get this prick away from me.*

It's the first time I get Piggy's name. Already, I can see she has some status in this place, and I'm glad she doesn't hear Luna properly.

*Luna, honestly, it wasn't me.*

*Doesn't take a scientist. Doesn't take Sherlock Holmes.*

*What?*

*It was you. I know it was you.* She's smiling dreamily, eyes doped, half closed. Mouth half open. Her hair falls across her face and she doubles over, showing the slender shape of her back. I hold her up and feel an unusual something; part curiosity, part protection.

*Fuck you doin' here, Luna?* I ask again.

She puts a finger in my face. *Fuck YOU doing here, Robin? You window breaker ... you ... heart breaker, window smasher ... my dad's gonna smash your face when ...*

I try to hold her up, but her body spills through my arms.

Just then, Kimberly returns; a wedge between us, a wall. The round blonde thing, and again I try to work out this too-familiar face. Luna and Kimberly. Beauty and the Beast. Beast laughs hard and dead-arms me with a short jab.

*No fucking, you two*, she says. *Unless I watch.*

Kimberly keeps making these comments about watching. She seems fixated.

Stepping away, looking at Luna, light in my arms.

She puts the white powder under our noses, first Luna then me.

*Fuck is this stuff?* I say.

Before I get an answer, it rockets right through me. A smooth, powerful rush; and it might be coke after all. All is good. All is gold.

*Fucking golden.*

A superhuman charge. Hint of sex now on the knife-edge of delicious violence.

Whip out my phone.

Boz:

*I'm ready. cunt. Eclipse.*
*Come NOW.*


### 'Dooms Night' by Azzido Da Bass

wallops through the speakers. A sonic boomerang of sound. That revolving *whaauumm*, like landing on a car roof, followed by smashing glass echoing down an endless well. The track pulls us all together, giving us a second wind. Arms up in unison, whipping over heads, like a lasso. She dances –

Luna.

*Luna Vallillo.*

Luna Vallillo of the Vallillos.

The Vallillo Family, the enemy.

How did she end up here? I'm still not convinced this is real.

The Holographic Universe, remember?

She's dancing with me. Up against me. Her soft yellow dress, wrapping her sultry sweat-beaded skin. She bites her dark lip, wrinkles her nose. In her own world yet owning mine. I watch her in amazement, in gorgeous awe.

*Dooms Night* drones on, an epic extended version with no end, and I don't want it to. I could listen to this track and watch this girl for the next thousand years.

Just then, I clock Kimberly on the edge of the dance floor, staring at us intensely, intently. Like she's had a plan all along.

She comes over.

*Go then. Kiss her.*

A small shove in my back and I almost fall right through Luna. She catches me somehow and I put my lips up to hers. She won't stop smiling. The kiss starts small and awkward, before slowly opening up and deepening. Swelling, sensual lips. Strawberry sweet.

I feel something take to the back of my head, unpleasant, like a huge tarantula gripped at my skull. Kimberly's hand is there. I note the bust knuckles and the raw, bitten nails. I try to block it out with Luna's exotic curves, which sway beneath me.

Kimberly is saying shit now. *You only fuck her when I say so. You do nothing without me.*

Then it sounds like she says something like *corruption* or *disruption*.

*C'mon.*

She seems to take both Luna and me away from the music and away from the floor. Out the door and down the stairs. Says goodbye to everyone in the club. Someone gives her something on the way out, and an uneasy feeling slams into me. A big black boy makes a grab at Luna, but Kimberly casually slaps his arm away. We walk the bare bricked corridor, and a taxi appears at the end of it. The battered doorway, a horrible morning mouth of cruel, cruellest delight, daylight. I feel a comedown even though I'm still full of buzz. Almost like the sight of morning is a reminder of what's to come.

We ride the cab. In the back between the two girls. Window open a little bit, blowing Luna's down-the-back brunette. She closes her eyes and feels the morning on her face. Her lashes hold the light. I start to see people appear on the street and can't believe how many are still up ... but then I realise ... *this is a new day.*

I feel the slow crawl of evil.

Of not being able to sleep of not being able to think of not being able to shut off from thinking.

Now it's more than just booze I have to deal with.

Kimberly seems to sense this and puts the bag back under my nose. The driver says something, but Kimberly tells him to *mind his fucking business.* She really is a ferocious piece of work. A force to be reckoned with. In me, I feel that warped admiration that I always have for people like this. Kimberly is in obvious control of the night, this morning. Luna. Me.

And I don't quite know where all this is going.

I'm definitely not safe.

The cab stops at a red light and really I should bail. Only Luna purrs next to me, and I know I'm not going anywhere. I feel like Kimberly is using her as some kind of weapon, *bait*.

Kimberly orders the cab driver about. Still pissed off with him for having the cheek to tell her not to do drugs in *his* car. He too is now under her control.

*Pull over here.*

Like with everything else of this night, I kind of recognise this street but not quite. A billboard and a terrace and a kid's play park.

*You broke my window*, Luna mumbles as she falls from the car.

I hold her up and walk her, all the time following Kimberly, who seems oddly clear-headed and centred, and I wonder if she's even taken any drugs herself.

This notion now fills me with full paranoia.

I'm wondering what I'm walking into. Rottweilers. Perverts. A gang of lads.

Someone holding a video camera. Someone with a wad of cash. More drugs.

Instinct screaming out loud now, *Run, take off.*

Yet the sway of Luna's arse has me following them all the way to the front door.

*How'd you two know each other then?*

Kimberly doesn't answer, just pulls open a beat-up door and into her yard we go. A scruffy shithole. I can't understand why Luna isn't fazed by this. Her family are loaded and stylish, big expensive cars, huge house in Woodthorpe.

*Why the fuck is she here?*

Kimberly gives me *more drugs*, only it's not doing much to me now. Just turning me into a wired vegetable. At last, I see her have a blast herself, and this eases me somewhat.

She turns the TV on and the three of us crash. She pulls a curtain, closing off that demon sunlight. Suddenly the shitpad starts to feel safe and I unwind a bit. Kimberly sits opposite and watches Luna as she puts her smooth brown legs across me.

*How do you two know each other*? I ask again.

*Can I have a cup of tea*? Luna suddenly says in a baby voice.

*Work*, Kimberly says, sparking up a fag. *How do YOU two know each other*? she says.

*Work.*

*Cup of tea*, Luna says again.

*You know where the kettle is, bitch.*

Luna has her lip out, and it's the first time I realise how fucked she is. Her eyes are rolling and she keeps doing this weird nodding thing.

*Hey, you all right*? I say.

She looks up at me like it's the first time she's seen me tonight.

*I wanna see you two kiss*, Kimberly says, enchanted.

Now out of the club, in her own home, Kimberly has softened some. Her hair looks lighter, her features clearer. Her eyes are a blatant blue. I note the kids' toys everywhere, crayon drawings stuck to the walls.

*You got kids?*

She nods although not really listening, just fixated on Luna and her legs and the way she is arched back on the threadbare sofa.

*Kiss*, she says impatiently.

*Well, okay then*, Luna whispers playfully.

I'm surprised at her sudden forwardness, sits right up and into me. Her head clumsily knocking against mine. We kiss, again. Same slow start, into something deep and luxurious. I hear Kimberly move around, becoming aroused. We carry on and on.

*Your clothes smell*, Luna laughs, pulling a face.

I laugh too. *I know*, I say. My days have been long. She's right. I need go shower.

I pull at my dark blue shirt, which now clings to me like a second skin.

*Yes, shower*, Kimberly says. *You both need to shower.*

To feel nerves and numbness at the same time, and to be so turned on on top of it all. Yet I'm so addled by everything that I'm not sure if I even have a dick anymore.

Luna can't make the stairs and Kimberly has to pretty much carry her the whole way. Noise and voices outside, and still I have no idea if this is midweek or weekend. Upstairs in Kimberly's crib. There is a main bedroom and a kid's room and a bathroom.

*Where's ya kid*? I find myself asking from nowhere.

*Fuckin' nosy you are, aren't ya.*

Kimberly throws Luna up the last few stairs and she falls immediately to the floor, into a small ball. She pulls at a chord and the shower sounds through the whole flat.

*In*, she says.

*What?*

*Kit off and in.*

She starts to unbutton my shirt, more practical than seductive. She holds my hips and turns me in the mirror.

*I like skinny*, Kimberly says. *Skinny is hot on a man. You're just what I wanted.*

I step in the shower and wash away. Face full in the beams. I reach over for some toothpaste and squeeze it into my mouth, foaming it up and spitting it out. Kimberly watches me.

*Why aren't you hard?* she says.

I vaguely remember last night, which now seems a week ago. My failed attempt at *fuck*. Kimberly reaches over and takes me in her grip, slowly growing in the palm of her hand. Relief at my manhood being restored.

Luna is still on the floor.

Kimberly lifts her up and takes off her dress.

Neither of us can believe our eyes. Only time I have ever seen a body like this is in porn.

*Fuck*, Kimberly gasps. *Fuck, are you even real?*

Luna has not a clue; she just stumbles around the landing knock-kneed. Kimberly has to guide her into the shower, wincing as the water hits her, surprising her skin.

*Hot, cold*, she says.

*Dooms Night* is still going through my head, echoing around this manky bathroom. The cracked tiles. Strands of matted hair clogged in the plughole. Clipped toenails. A blue plaster taped to the wall. Scab of shit in the toilet. Luna and I are crowded in this ridiculous space and Kimberly watches on.

*Kiss her then, suck on her tits.*

I look at Luna fully in the face. The steam rises.

I look at Luna in the face and realise she's not there, not here.

*Suck those fucking nipples. Do as I say.*

Kimberly kicks off her jeans and puts the lid down on the toilet. One of her chunky legs slams on the bath.

*Suck 'em then.*

Luna's large breast, large areola. The whole of her impossibly slender and voluptuous at the same time. Yet when I look at her face, all my desire drains away cos she's simply not there. Her eyes are gone. She is empty.

She nods and falls, slurs, hums. Occasionally, she snaps out of it, and when she does, there is pure fright and disorientation.

*We need to get her out of here*, I say suddenly.

Kimberly's hand is deep into her own pussy now, frigging herself off. Her eyes lose concentration as the meaning of my words sets in.

*What?*

*We need to get this girl dried, clothed, watered and put to bed.*

*Fuck you talking about, ya freak?*

I soften and shorten, and this goddess bod means nothing to me now. Nothing to me now in *that way*.

I cover her and carry her out.

Kimberly gets desperate. The red on her face, the wet on her fingers.

*She wants to, she wants to. She kissed you, for fuck's sake. She's consenting. It's consensual.*

The use of these words makes it all the more real.

Kimberly still ain't giving up. *Just ... take her to my bed and fuck her.*

I take her to the bed, wrapping her, towelling her, looking into her eyes, which are closing by the passing of seconds. *You got a t-shirt or something? Pass me a t-shirt.*

*This night is fucking lame*, Kimberly says.

She pulls open a drawer and throws a huge turquoise American football top at me, the number 12 smacking me in the face. Luna is now unconscious and it's like the first time Kimberly is acknowledging all this. She stomps around her flat, naked from the waist down, fully clothed on top.

I dry Luna gently, her neck, her hair. Even her toes.

Miami Dolphins is two sizes too big and buries her. The aqua colours brilliant against her flawless Italian complexion.

*You're not fucking real*, Kimberly says. *You know you'll never get this chance again, don't you.*

*Kimberly*, I say. *She's fucking passed out.*

*Not really she wasn't ... I mean ... only cos you let her ... only cos you let her sleep ... if you'd have just sucked her ...*

I manage to get Luna's knickers back on then carry her to the bed.

*Nah*, Kimberly says. *That's my bed. Take her to the kid's room.*

I carry her along the small landing. A Buzz Lightyear duvet cover with a Sleeping Beauty pillowcase, and I can't work out if it's a boy's room or a girl's room. I put her in and wrap her up. Fetch her some water. For a moment, she stirs and looks at me. Right at me. I try to find something in her eyes, some deeper meaning, but all in all it's just a girl who needs to sleep.

When I get back to Kimberly, she's looking a certain way and I try to work it out. The nearest I can find is nerves. She's nervous for some reason and maybe even fear and the first hint of vulnerability all night.

She's moving around, a sort of squirming, still touching her pussy.

*You know you need to fuck me.*

I'm wrecked, tender, scared to death and with no arousal at all, yet the thought of rejecting Kimberly in this moment seems impossible. She's close to the edge and that puts me on the edge. We're both edging each other.

It's Kimberly's night and it's not gone her way.

She gets the sniff back out.

Something I thought I'd never say: *No more.*

She knows and nods and puts it away. Tosses it on the bedside table and moves up towards me.

*Can we just sleep?* I say, a little helplessly.

She shakes her head like it's not even an option. She goes on all fours, her huge rump in the dirty mirror, tattooed and not altogether clean. Yet the sight of it kicks something off in me. First real lust of the night. Kimberly takes me in her mouth and she's good at this. Better than I expected, softer than I imagined.

I look up and a burning orb of light looks back.

And then I kind of get a higher vision of the night. Of being here.

I feel the three lost souls in this tiny shithole of a house. The needs of us all, to be accepted by each other in whatever way. The changing needs, the shifting desires. To get high and get fucked, to get off and protect and be protected, to sleep and be safe, to *feel* something.

To get naked and hide at the same time.

*Take off your top,* I say.

*Fuck off,* she replies.

I'm inside her and I'm lucky cos I can tell she's gonna be a quick cumer. Already the sounds and the shudders, this whole night of voyeuristic charm has acted as the perfect foreplay for her. For once in my whole life, I'm more bothered about her orgasm than my own. By now, I just want it to end.

Give her what she needs so I can go sleep.

My own end is getting there too, building up and building up, sensations starting in my lower back, as the residual cocaine-tingles play at the nerve endings. Our orgasms head in the same direction. I look at her face. This face I have known all night but can't quite put my finger on ... *frighteningly familiar.* I kiss her hard on the mouth and her eyes soften a little, and for a moment I catch love there. Love behind her aggression and control and ego.

This love cos she knows I am a good man or that I have *some* goodness, *somewhere*, and she has seen this tonight.

*I'm a lesbian that fucks the odd guy*, she mysteriously says out of nowhere.

And for some reason I get fixated on the word *odd.*

Does she mean odd as in *few* or odd as in *strange*?

*I'm ready to cum now*, she gasps.

*Me too*, I say.

*Together*, she says, gripping my neck.

Something so sad, and desperate and beautiful and confusing to all this.

With a second until lift-off and this face of hers suddenly makes sense. This harsh wide face, pinkish, piggy.

And her full name, which I saw on an envelope downstairs ... *Kimberly Wilkinson ... Wilkinson ... WILKinson ... Wilk ... Wilk ... Little Ron Wilk ... fuck ... NO ... YES ... I'm cummin' ... no ... yes ... NOOOOO.*

Day Four
# The Fall

'I love life – that's my real weakness. I love it so much that I am incapable of imagining what is not life.'

Albert Camus, *The Fall*

# Fallen

As always with drugs, going for a piss that never comes.

Kimberly snores, nostrils flapping.

I stand there and I stand there, sore dick in my hand, staring at the scab of shit on the side of the toilet. *Aiming* at the scab of shit. The piss feeling is overwhelming but it just won't come. For the first time, I notice the mess in my mouth. Tonguing the inside of my cheek, the tears and the blood-bubbles, the swelling gums and already-formed ulcers.

Not normally a cocaine thing but a Mandy thing.

The drug in question. The mystery of the white powder.

Full daylight now and everyday life moves outside the window. Kids, buses.

Just then, a figure at the door. Instinctively, I pull my boxers back up.

Luna standing there with one sock on. Her brown knee against the white doorframe, Miami Dolphins slacked to one side, her smooth shoulder, shining. Her hair hanging over her face. I can barely see her eyes.

*What happened?* she says.

*What do you mean?* I ask.

She hangs her head.

*Oh, nothing,* I say.

I'm looking all around the bathroom and Luna is looking at the floor. She moves her toes.

*Where's Kimberly?*

*Asleep,* I say.

*Will you ... will you come talk to me a bit.*

I nod, and we shuffle into the kid's room.

Under Buzz Lightyear, over Sleeping Beauty.

The single has us close and she curls up and nestles into my chest.

Nothing but soothing silence for maybe an hour or more. No sleep, though.

Occasionally, we take sips from the pint of tap water that I had left last night. The parched, ravaged inside of my mouth turns the liquid into a nasty battery taste, and by the look on Luna's face the same is happening to her.

*Ugh,* she says, *never again.*

At last, we can bear to face each other. A pair of dilated pupils gazing into a pair of dilated pupils.

*You wanna knock this drug shit on the head before it starts, Luna. I'm not even kidding.*

*I've always wanted to try it,* she says in a small voice.

*Well ... you've tried it.*

Her warm body under me yet still not a hint of desire. Our legs tangle and it feels so nice.

*You need to stay away from her as well,* I say.

*Hey, she's my best friend.*

A sudden robust emotion, which surprises me.

*How long you known her?*

*Coupla months.*

*Yeah, well,* I make an effort to keep my voice down, *she's fuckin' dangerous and she's related to dangerous people, and you need to stay away.*

She seems to listen, her eyes on the ceiling, blinking fast.

She grips me a little tighter and makes herself smaller. Her hair in my face.

I look down at her and then something starts to come over me.

The feeling of falling.

This happens to me every couple of years and is without a doubt connected to the booze and everything else.

The feeling of falling.

The fear of falling.

Normally with girls just out of reach.

Girls like ...

Luna.

We kiss and wrap. I start to notice more about her in this morning light. As her make-up breaks away and her true face appears. Smallness of her nose. Largeness of her eyes. Mole on her neck. Certain shape her mouth makes when she's concentrating on something. I always liked her at work. Of all the Vallillos, she was the best one. And not just cos of the way she looks but her warmth and quirky humour and her cute cluelessness to everything, her *away-with-the-fairies* dreaminess.

Now she's in my arms.

140

*If I shouldn't be here then you shouldn't be here*, she says, suddenly.

*What do you mean?* I ask.

For a moment, I wonder if she's talking in her sleep cos her eyes are about to go.

I watch them and let them, her eyes getting heavier and heavier and mine do too.

My ears pick up the faint chime of a siren, then we both fall, fall asleep at the same time. Or so it seems.


## Butterfly Kisses

I wake but don't open my eyes fully. Putting a sprinkle of butterfly kisses over this arm that lays on top of my arm. Her hair is all over me and I feel the wonder of this king-size sleep, which may have just erased all trace of hangover and comedown. This naked body of a new love is the new start I need in life. To fix it and go forward. To sober up and heal and enter something bigger than myself. Being with *someone else*.

I kiss this skin again, but it seems to pull away a bit.

I open my eyes and look at the skin; colder, harder, whiter.

*Fuck you doin', ya drip?*

I sit up and look up.

*Don't start getting all soppy, ya prick.*

I look into Luna's face but it isn't Luna's face.

It's another face.

It's the face belonging to


## Li'l Ron Wilk's Daughter

*We've still got some of that stuff left, y'know*, she says.

In her fingers is the white bag, near full.

*What the fuck is that stuff anyway?*

*Ching.*

*What's with all the rushy feelings then?*

She shrugs.

*Must have been boshed up to fuck.*

*Fuck off, my stuff's ten-ten.*

*Hmm.*

*It was that pill you popped.*

*I didn't pop no pill.*

*Yeah, you did. I got it for you.*

I feel around in my mouth, licking through the sores.

*C'mon*, she says.

I hear the sniff from Kimberly and she then hands me the bag. I hold it. I don't want it.

Yet I know I need it, and this is the last thing I fucking wanted.

*Where's Luna?*

Kimberly kneels up and inspects herself in the mirror. *Fucked off ages ago.*

I snort.

My mind is in bits. I can't work out what's happened. I can't work out what's real, what's dream, what I've imagined. The falling feeling is still there and I feel that little dark girl at the centre of my chest, under all this chaos, booze and class As. A fear that Kimberly might try and fuck me again starts up, but I notice she is different now. Her mannerisms more manly, and she moves around differently and relates to me more as a mate. The resemblance to her old man is freakishly uncanny, and I can't believe I didn't clock this last night.

*Where do you know Luna from again?*

*Oh, stop fuckin' goin' on about her. She's done one, end of.*

Speech a dead ringer to her dad's as well.

*She's just some lame I keep knocking about. She serves a purpose. Don't go getting loved-up like they all do. Won't do you any good.*

More characteristics of her dad. Sounding thick as fuck but streetwise to the letter. A head for head games, power dynamics, sniffing out weakness. Dangerous.

*We gettin' back on it or what?*

She seems embarrassed that my cock has been in her. Even with the sniff back in the system she won't look in my eyes, but I'm in no hurry with that one, either.

The coke has done little for me.

Think I'm reaching the point where my body is in full rejection of all toxics. It's a horrible place to be in. In need of escape but nothing will go in. This may well be my *hitting of the wall.*

I feel sick.

I feel lovesick.

The longing is so powerful it sits in the driver's seat of this comedown.

The thought of Luna gone is debilitating. I can see her face and hear her voice and smell her skin. A strand of brunette lays across my naked knee.

I find myself strategising on ways to find her, save her, love her. I think of the restaurant. I think of where she still lives with her mum and dad. That huge house in Woodthorpe. I must write her a letter. Send it in the post. Old school. Romantic.

I take the strand of her hair and put it in my wallet.

*Oh my God, I know that prick,* Kimberly says loudly, pointing at the telly. *He went my school.*

*Jeremy Kyle* is on and Kimberly is stood, smiling, watching it.

There's a red-headed lad standing on stage, offering the audience out. *Yo, any of you lot wanna come step to me solo?*

Kimberly lets out a sharp snort of laughter. *Step to me solo, ha. Who fuckin' sez that anymore? He was a prick at school and he's a prick now. I once belted him in the mouth in maths.*

### Lucy Kite

For some reason, she depresses me today. There's something cruel in her expression. She mocks. She *gloats*. She can see through the TV. She can see *me*. She can see the state I'm in and the state I'm with – this beast, this beat-up gangster lesbian. She can see the room I'm in. She can smell the drugs, the shit. That dirty feel to everything. The *grime*.

After this weather report, Lucy Kite will be picked up by her sports-star boyfriend. A footballer, no, a rugby player. Big and handsome and successful and rich. They will drive out in their Audi TT to their big house in the near-country; Ruddington, Edwalton or, even better, Bunny. Where he will have a healthy meal cooked for her. A glass of expensive wine but no more. Their relationship based on moderation, monogamy and mutual respect. He will take her to bed at a reasonable hour and make slow love to her between the satin sheets, sight of the rolling hills in the distance. Making love and making children.

Family, future, fruits of labour and the good, good life.

Kimberly belches beside me. Hoovers up another line.

Gives me one.

We're downstairs now.

*Who cares, skinny bitch*, Kimberly screams at the screen. A smiling Lucy wishing us all *a pleasant day.*

*Look out the window if you wanna know the weather. It's raining. Yesterday, sun. Today, fucking rain. This is the Midlands and it's bollocks. And we don't need no kebab-dodging anorexic bitch to tell us that.*

### 'Loose Women'

We sit for a bit. Watching the same shit TV I watch at Fry's.

Kimberly fucks around on her phone.

Then,

she coughs.

Then,

she says:

*Dad's coming round in a minute. Drop me some dollar off and then we'll get back on it. Fancy doin' Mapperley Top?*

### Wilk

Life flashing before me. I see it all playing out. Wilk walking through the front door. Walking into this room. The shock on his face. The fear on mine. Fuck knows what he'll do after that. Fuck knows what he'll do to *me*. Not sticking around to find out.

I'm on my feet.

*Where's nearest shop?*

*Carlton Hill. Why?*

*Get some warm-up tins, innit?*

*Fuck that. He'll be here in a minute.*

Sweat from every pore. Trying to hide the sheer terror I'm currently hijacked by.

*He'll drop us off up Mapperley Top*, she says. *Might have to pop in the Cavo for one with the fat old cunt but that's all right.*

My paranoid ears are picking up all the sounds now: an engine, a car door, footsteps down the path.

I'm literally seconds from bolting.

*Nah, wanna pick up some other bits*, I say, a detectable quiver in my voice.

*Like what?*

She's scraping her hair back into a bun. Something suspicious in her eye contact.

*Just … bits*, I say.

*Well, don't be long*, she snaps. *My dad ain't a waiting-around-for-cunts kind of person.*

I nod, hand already on the handle, but it won't budge. This hand is shaking and Kimberly spots this as she comes over and unlocks the door, pushing it down, releasing it, setting me free.

I step outside.

*Oh and, Robin.*

*Yeah.*

*If this is you backdooring it … then I'll take it very personal … and you will be on my list.*

*Yeah, right*, I say, smiling.

Her unbeatable eye contact ends only when she decides to. With a sly, subtle yet very real *wink*.


### Check Ya Mate

Check my phone at the top of Standhill Road.

Missed calls.
Thirteen of them.

Three from Cassidy.
Three from Boz.
Seven from Boss.

*Boss.* The full horror of last night. Darren in a pool of blood. Piss and shit and vomit. Police cars. Ambulance. A big court case. A media frenzy. Splashed all over the newspapers. Front page. CQC.

Care home closed. Prison sentence. Life sentence. Death sentence. Then I remember the underage girls and their fathers. Sex Offenders List. Vigilante mobs.

Nowhere to run nowhere to hide.

Checkmate.

I'm fucked, man.

A fucked man.

Fucked it, proper.

Proper fucked it this time.

Time to leave.

Time to roll time to flex time to drop-shoulder and bounce.

Time to get out of

## Nottingham

Never thought there'd be a point when I had to leave but this is it. Pack my bags and go. On a bus on a plane. Cadge a lift. I need to leave need to go. Midnight run *Midnight Express*. Disappear into a tunnel of stars. Hiding in smoke. Lose myself in London. One of them little urban villages. *Swiss Cottage. St John's Wood. White City.* Go QPR games on a Saturday.

Forgotten Forest. Forgottingham.

Or maybe somewhere up north.

Meet and settle with a girl in Wigan or Doncaster. A girl with a kid, to be a ready-made dad.

Or move myself to the coast and live alone. By the sea. The flatlands and Badlands of Lincolnshire. That little town of Kimble Wells with the Clementine Channel running through it, under rickety bridges. Build a life out there. A make-believe America.

## The Free Man

I step in this pub, which could be stupid cos it's the first place Wilk and Daughter Wilk could come. The nearest watering hole. Another Wetherspoons. I think about Freud and his theory of the death drive, the myth of Thanatos. Yep, I agree with the bearded Austrian cunt. Cos what other explanation is there as to why I've done what I've done in the last four days. Building myself a road that leads right to my grave.

The bar.

All this going on and still the devil manages to smile at me. She is bottle tanned and silicone titted. Bosom buddy. GILF with her wrinkled hand wrapped around a pump, ready to pull me one.

I talk to her and flirt with her as if nothing in the world was wrong.

As if this was a completely normal day, not one where I have killed a retard and have half the city looking for me.

She calls me *darling* and tells me the price and I pull out my wallet of moths.

*ATM in here, good-lookin'?*

*Just in the corner, handsome.*

I point at the rising bubbles inside my Strongbow. *I'll be back*, I say, in full Schwarzenegger.

GILF laughs and my mind wanders and wonders if I've fucked a woman as old as this. I leaf through the pages of my mental fuck book. Absentmindedly, Barclays slides into the hole in the wall. Punch in my pin. Punch in thirty quid. Do I accept the charge? Yes, I do. The little box of cash hums as I think of the next chat-up line to use on GILF. When I turn back around, the screen has two words glaring right at me.

### Insufficient Funds

Some mistake, I immediately think. Only got paid yesterday, so some mistake, some error on *their* part. The bank the system the bigger picture. Panic now dread now doom. Thoughts overtaking themselves. I look back at the bar as GILF is serving someone else. Mr Strongbow sitting on the bar. Waiting for me.

Barclays back in. Try twenty try ten. And still.

Insufficient. Funds.

I bite through my teeth and feel a rage so strong I want to put my head through the wall. Or more this ATM. Smash this into smithereens and do us both some damage. For a moment, my suspicions turn on Kimberly. What if she fished out my card in the night? Taken down my details and passed them on. *Nah, don't be stupid.* Next, my mind goes through the financial activity of the last couple of days. The epic rounds. The top-shelf spending. Shaun of the Dead must have had fifty off me *at least*. Suddenly my rage is turned in on him. That dirty leech taking advantage of my good nature. Wilk warned me but I didn't listen. I feel like jumping on the 25 bus into town. Track the tramp and get my money back. Beat it from him. Now my hangover is in full swing. Coke comedown cornering my consciousness.

I head back to the bar.

*All right, sweetheart.*

GILF looks at me through her glasses. She senses something is wrong.

I put my hand on Strongbow before she has a chance to take it away.

*Sorry,* I say.

*Oh, you little bastard.*

I grab and run, spilling most of it down my front.

GILF is hot on my heels. I feel her smack me around the back of the head.

Now I'm laughing my head off. Laughing full pelt.

Dodging in and out of chairs, dancing around her as I drink.

She grabs at me claws at me.

I'm saturated in cider. Some comes up through my nose.

Out onto the street and I down it as fast and as hard as I can. A bubble breaks over my face and strings of goo hang from my mouth.

*You're fucking barred. Don't show your face around here again.*


## Cassidy

*You need to lend me twenty quid.*
*What?*
*Nowt.*
*Robin?*
*Cassidy.*
*Robin, where the fuck you been?*
*What?*
*Been calling you for days. Why the fuck you not been picking up?*
*You know why.*
*Fuck's sake, Robin.*
*Look, it's just the way it is.*
*Way what is?*

*It's just the way it is for now.*
*Fuck does that mean?*
*It won't last forever.*
*What won't?*
*This.*
*What's this?*
*Look, I need twenty.*
*No way.*
*Just put it into my account, will ya.*
*No.*
*Just this once.*
*It's never just this once.*
*Just—*
*It was this once five years ago.*
*This once.*
*It was this once last week and it'll be this once next week.*
*I've met a girl, Cassidy, and this time I'm gonna do it right.*
*A girl is the last thing you need.*
*Her name is—*
*It's a girl that put you there in the first place.*
*You can't blame Mum.*
*I'm not blaming Mum.*
*You always mention her, but she's got fuck all to do with it.*
*I'm not mentioning Mum. I never mentioned Mum.*
*Good cos—*
*She came out of your lips, not mine.*
*I—*
*You came out of her vagina, not mine.*
*You—*
*I can't look after you forever, Robin.*
*You don't look after me.*
*I can't worry about you forever, Robin.*
*You barely leave the house.*
*I've got my own life to live.*
*FUCKING LIVE IT THEN.*

Silence.

I see Kimberly and her dad pass in a white van.
    I hold my breath and hide in a phone box while on the phone.

*Look, Cassidy, have you heard owt?*
*'Bout what?*
*'Bout me?*
*Like what?*
*Anything.*
*Robin, you're worrying me now.*
*Look, no, it's nothing …*
*You're really scaring me now, Robin.*
*Cassidy, calm down. I didn't mean it to sound like that.*
*You sound weird. Really weird. Even weirder than normal.*
*I'm fine.*
*You been on the bag?*
*No.*
*You been on the sniff?*
*No.*
*Please don't lie to me, Robin. That's all I ask. Please don't lie to me.*
*I've been on the sniff.*
*Oh fuck.*
*Just a little. Just one night.*
*Is that what you want the dollar for?*
*No.*
*What do you want the dollar for?*

I think about lying to her. I think about manipulating her.

I contemplate saying I owe big men and then she'll have to cough up, but that really is a horrible thing to do to your sister. Your own flesh and blood.

It's a horrible thing to do to anyone.

*I just need another drink.*
*Thought you got paid yesterday?*
*Just enough for a few. Just enough to bring me down. I'm at the end now, I can tell.*

*Come here*, she yelps.

The desperation in her voice does something to me.

*Come here*, she repeats. *Come here. Rattle off here. I'll make you a bed up. Give you space. Give you soup. Give you a new razor. I'll keep the dogs away. Make sure they won't bother you. I know you hate that. We can watch all your favourite films, the comfort films you always watch when coming off.* Back to the Future, *that* Ferris

Bueller *bollocks. Come home, Robin. I'll even get you a few cans to ease you off with. A bottle of slow red wine.*

I step out from the phone box.

The late-afternoon traffic is building now, kids on buses, that just-before-rush-hour atmosphere.

*All right*, I say.

*You will?*

*Yeah*, I say.

All of her street-edge is gone now. Her voice soft and young.

Like the little sister I've always known.

*You promise?* she says one last time.

*I promise*, I say.


### Sherwood Rise

I climb up to his window, *Dawson's Creek*-style.

Three little taps and then his face appears. So much muck on the glass I can barely make him out.

Wiping his eyes. *Robin, fuck you doin'?*

*Fry, please tell me you're holding.*

*What?*

Fry lives in a crackhead rehab unit. He's strictly not allowed visitors.

He looks around, scared.

*You know I can't have people here unless they're on the list, bruv. You'll get me thrown out.*

I spot the green bottle by his bed. The label half-picked off: WHITE STORM.

*Open up. I'm coming in.*

Strangely, he doesn't protest.

*Not much security in this crackhead business, is there.*

*Don't say that, bruv. Don't mock me.*

I take his storm of White and gulp it hard.

*Fuckin' hell, Robin.*

We pass the bottle back and forth and life gets better. Sitting at opposite sides of his broken bed. Damp patch on the ceiling. Bottles and butts everywhere. Pot Noodles of every flavour in every corner of this tiny room.

*Fuck off. You never had a threesome.* His eyes go wide and childish.

151

*I swear on my …*

His eyes go even bigger and I stop myself before finally saying … *sister's life.*

*A threesome?*

*One of them was a model.*

*Nofuckingway.*

*An Italian model … I'm taking her on a date next week.*

*Lucky bastard.*

I nod my head while drinking the bottle.

*I mean, you've always been good with girls, Robin, but—*

*Her body, my God. Had her in the shower. Never known owt like it.*

Fry suddenly hangs his head. Sad-eyed. *See, bruv, that's what I want. Not sex really, just love off a beautiful girl. Someone like Cheryl—*

Cutting him off before he starts his boring bollocks about Cheryl Cole.

*If I could have a girl like that, I'd turn my life around.*

*Let's go out!* I say, I sing.

*Drug worker says it's cos I'm getting my emotions back.*

*Let's go on a raise before it gets dark.*

*And do what, go where?*

*Well, we've arranged to meet those girls, haven't we?*

*What girls?*

*Cheryl Cole and Scarlett Johansson. Double date, remember?*

For a moment, I swear I see a rat disappear under Fry's bed.

*You're off your fuckin' head, bruv.*

*Scarlett's just text. They've just got on the Pronto at Mansfield. Told her we'd meet them up at the Arboretum. Said we'd pick up another bottle of White Storm for each couple. You and Chez and me and Scar. So look lively. They want to watch the sunset with us.*

Fry is scratching his head. White scalp dust falls like snow. *Do you think they'd agree to THAT?*

*Oh sure*, I say.

He's laughing now.

*You do know how to cheer me up, ya nutter.*

*C'mon*, I say on standing. *We need to earn some money before it gets dark.*

## On a Raise

Fry and I have different ways in which we raise. Different methods. Fry is sly and tricky, uses sob stories and sleights of hand. Distraction techniques and bamboozling language. Whereas I just go straight in for the kill.

*Not gonna bullshit you. I'm struggling at the minute and I've turned to drink. Could you spare a quid so I can buy a bottle? You'd be a legend if you could help me out. Hook a brother up. I'd remember you for life.*

Sometimes, it worked. Sometimes, it made them laugh. Sometimes, they said the honesty was *refreshing*, and it would often spark a stimulating conversation. Then they'd end up giving me *even* more money. This evening, I raised fifteen quid in under an hour. Better than minimum wage. Doubling Fry. Armed with a 2-litre each, we step through the university entrance of the Arboretum.

A scarecrow of an old man stands by the gates, sporting a matching City Council hat and shirt.

*Closing in twenty, lads.*

*Just passing through, sir*, I say.

*No problem, mate.*


## Cheryl & Scarlett

A fictionalised sunset breaks over the paper trees.

Turning the world orange.

An ink-splatter of birds flies through it.

Fry looks around with a child's searching wonder. *How can you not believe in God, with beauty like this?*

*All right, gals!* I suddenly shout, aiming my voice over the hills.

Fry raises onto his tiptoes, confused.

*Here they are*, I say.

*Who?*

*Who'd ya think?*

*Fuck you on about?*

*Up by the war cannons.*

Fry moves into the open space.

*There's no one there.*

*Are you blind?* I point. *They're coming towards us, NOW.*

*You're on summat, bruv.*

*Blonde, brunette. Told ya they'd come.*

*Who?*

*Scarlett and Cheryl.*

*You're off your fucking head!*

*Come here*, I say to him, all the time looking over his shoulder at the girls.

I straighten Fry's collar. Lick my thumb, wiping Pot Noodle from his chin.

*Now*, I begin, *don't be shy. Just relax and treat them like any other girl. Don't let fame and beauty intimidate you. I don't know the last time you went on a double date, or any date for that matter, but be a gentleman. I'll talk first and then you follow my lead.*

Fry finds himself nodding, going into some kind of trance.

*Scarlett, Cheryl*, I say coolly. *Glad you could make it. You both look wonderful this evening.*

I take Scarlett by the hand, kiss her on the cheek.

*Fry*, I say, *Cheryl is waiting for your arm.*

He's staring into space, moving forward. Suddenly he opens up an arm.

*That's it. Cheryl, you take his arm. You'll have to excuse him. He's a little shy tonight. Never been one for the big occasion, have you, Friar Tuck?*

The four of us disappear under the stone bridge, turning my voice into an echo.

*Is this a beautiful sunset or what, Ms Johansson? The best, right? Bet you don't get sunsets like this in the States, do you?*

We walk by the bird cages. Scarlett and I stop to take a look at the colourful creatures while Cheryl and Fry hang back. Fry with his head down while Cheryl does all the talking.

*Gorgeous, aren't they?* I whisper in her ear.

*You're off your fucking head!* Fry cries out.

*Language, Fry. The girls don't wanna hear this kind of talk. Do you, babe?*

Scarlett bites her lip, gives her head a little shake.

*See*, I say. *Sorry, Cheryl. It must be the nerves. I've got to say that most of the time he is a true gent ... let's keep walking ... for instance, it's no secret that Fry is totally loved up with you, Cheryl. But, you know, when he talks about you, it's with the utmost respect. Your eyes.*

*That's the big one. He's always going on about your eyes. For ages, I thought he was saying arse. You know, because of his accent. 'Cheryl's got the best arse.' When I said this to him, he quickly corrected me. 'It's EYES. Cheryl's got the best EYES.' It's quite beautiful the way he talks about you. Pure, you know. He loves you way better than that husband of yours. But, hey, we're not talking about him tonight. It's just the four of us now, yeah?*

I turn my attention to my date.

*You see, Scarlett, I used to see you in the same light ... back in the days of* Ghost World *and* Lost in Translation. *But ever since your hot little role in that shit Woody Allen film, I haven't been able to look at you the same. But we'll save that one for later, yeah?*

Scarlett blushes and looks the other way.

*Hey, Fry, why don't you tell Cheryl how long you've been clean?*

Scarlett and I have a few yards on the other couple.

At first, he doesn't say anything, so I have to shout after him again.

*Fry, how long?*

*Err, twenty-one, no, twenty-three days*, he manages.

*Tell her more, man. Tell her about it all. Hull. Prison. Grandma. Tell her what you're gonna do after you've weaned yourself off the booze. Tell her all the things you're gonna do with your new life.*

I pick up pace.

*Slow down*, Scarlett says, *can't walk fast in these heels.*

*Sorry but I need to give my boy space.*

I hear Fry start to talk, uncertain at first, but then it just pours all the way out of him. Full, flowing, like never before. His hopes, his dreams. Where he wants to live and what he's going to do. The ideas, the plans. His perfect job. Countries he wants to travel to. Learn a language, a musical instrument. Get fit and start playing football again. See his beloved baby nephew and maybe even have kids of his own one day. To hear him talk like this. To see a whole new side of him.

By the time we climb the gates at North Sherwood Street, Fry's a little out of breath.

His eyes are shimmering.

We help the girls down from the gate, taking their hands, lowering them gently onto the pavement.

*Well, girls, that was fuckin' beautiful. What a double date! Something none of us will ever forget.*

Fry is nodding his head.

*Scarlett*, I say, *your signature lips are even more sensational in real life, and, Cheryl ... Fry was right about your eyes ... it's most definitely ... been proven.*

Someone walking their dog looks at us gone-out. Fry hides away, embarrassed.

I take Scarlett into my arms and look deep into her eyes, kiss *those* lips. Goodbye.

Fry doesn't really say goodbye to his girl. He just sort of stands there with his hands in his pockets.

### An Off-licence in Sneinton

We walk in silence. Fry has sunk into his own world. There's a bit of a riot in the Old Dog & Partridge as we pass. I'm tempted to talk him into hitting this, but I know he won't wanna, and really I should leave him to his thoughts. He looks sad, confused. There is a *totally given-up* bearing to him that I haven't quite seen before. We walk by the Ice Arena where some boy band is playing. Excited teeny girls bounce about, full of joy. Fry walks through them; oblivious, numb.

The off-licence is a grimy little shack under a block of flats. A bleep sounds as we open the door and move on through to the bottles. The man behind the counter has one ready for us.

*Make that two*, I say.

The handsome Asian man smiles, running a thumb across his designer stubble.

*You want these bagging?*

*Can do, bruv.*

*Probably best*, he says. *Feds are getting funny about naked bottles on the streets these days.*

Fry has his head down, not taking any of it in. *How you been, bruv?* he says to the man.

*Oh, you know.* A sudden sadness sweeps across his face.

*Not seen you in ages*, Fry pushes on. *Where you been?*

*Too many funerals, brother.*

First time I notice the thickness of his Pakistani accent.

*What? Why? What you mean?*

I'm taken aback to see Fry break from his stupor. Suddenly there is lots of emotion.

*My brother, my father. Both in the same month.*

Fry drops his bottle to the floor and takes the man into his arms. The scene is alarming, and massively out of character.

*Oh, bruv, I'm so sorry. You know what … it's a hard fuckin' life. A HARD fuckin' life.*

The man is both wide-eyed and touched. Like he doesn't know what to do. Slowly, he takes himself out of Fry's embrace.

I'm feeling a little crazy myself. Edgy, addled. In need of a drink but that hitting the wall again. My brain feels like scrambled eggs. What I'm thinking and what I'm saying don't match. It's an awful, awful feeling. A crippling discord with the world.

Next, just a silent awkwardness as we three stand there, in this off-licence in Sneinton.

I get this panic to say something. Add to this scene, break the tension.

So I do.

*Which one bothers you the most?*

*Sorry,* says the man.

*Of the two deaths, which one bothers you the most?*

The man's face draws a blank and Fry's mouth falls open.

*Dad or brother, which one bothers you the most?*

*I mean—*

*Sorry, I don't know why I said that,* I say, putting my head down, pinching my nose.

*I mean, I can't really—*

*Sorry, I don't know what I'm saying.*

*I don't know how I'm expected to answer this.*

*D-d-don't answer this,* I stutter. *I'm just … completely—*

*Off your fucking head!* Fry jumps in, mouth still wide open.

*I'm sorry.*

*Robin, what the fuck are you on about?*

*It's the booze. I'm fucking up.*

I put a shaky hand to my head.

A pain so deep in Fry's chest. *This man has just told you that half his family is dead and you ask him which one is worse.*

*No, I never said it like that.*

The man stands up straight. *Can you both just leave.*

*You're off your fucking head!*

My head goes low. *Sorry,* I say to the man. *Sorry.*

Fry hangs back, apologising to the man, over-apologising to the man.

Once we're out of the off-licence, the *Open* sign is turned to *Closed*, and then there's the sound of the lock.

*What the fuck was that?*

Fry is shouting so much the noise travels through the iron stairwell of the flats.


## Bored Games

*What the fuck was that?*

*I didn't mean for it to sound like that.*

*How else was it meant to sound? The man's brother and dad have died and you ask him which one BOTHERS HIM THE MOST. Like he's supposed to pick. Like it's a flavour of ice cream or something.*

*What?*

*What kind of sick, twisted shit is that?*

*All right, calm down.*

I no longer know what we're arguing about.

I no longer know what is real.

From nowhere, I just find it all so funny. I fall into full hysteria.

*It's not fucking funny!*

*Which one bothers you most? Hahahaha. Which one bothers you most? Brother or dad? Hahahahaha.*

*You're off your fuckin' head.*

Feel like Fry has said that line a hundred times tonight. A million. You're off your fuckin' head.

I track him and shout on after him, *Which one bothers you most?*

*Stay away from me.*

Fry is striding across Sneinton Market, towards the Bath Inn.

*Which one bothers you the fuckin' most? Hahahahahaha.*

From nowhere, Fry stops and turns into me. For a moment, I think he might throw a punch.

*This is what you do, Robin. You play mind games with people. You say weird shit to try and shock people, get a reaction. Taking pleasure in other people's misfortunes. And all that bollocks at the Arboretum with the girls. Giving false hopes. Making fake promises. Trying to get in people's heads. MY head. Getting me to open up. Taking the piss. Taking the piss out of how I talk. You only keep me around to make yourself feel better. Cos I'm lower than you, aren't I? I mean there's not many lower than you, but I am. Scraping the scum of the barrel.*

*And you only want me when no one else is around. You're a using bastard. Well, no more, Robin. No more. Me and you are done.*

He moves five steps away.

*Fry.*

He turns.

*You know one thing that's always confused me about you,* I say.

His face is listening.

*Your grandma was cremated, right?*

How dare I mention her, his face says.

He nods with his eyes.

*So why the fuck do you always swear on her grave?*

Deep shock in his eyes. A twitch in his mouth.

I want him to smack me but he won't.

But for the first time ever I feel our power dynamic switch.

I am beneath him. Lower than Fry.

He walks calmly away, turning the corner, disappearing into St Ann's.


*Your grandma,* I shout after him, *bet she was a great fuck.*


### Nottingham Castle

I stash White Storm there.

By the Robin Hood statue, under one of the arches in the castle walls. I make a mental note on where exactly, remembering that disturbing scene with Jack Lemmon in the film *Days of Wine and Roses.*

Fuck this hobo shit, drinking in the streets. That's for the likes of losers like Fry.

I'm a man of the people. An aficionado of the human experience.

An individual of high art and charisma. The Dylan Thomas of Nottingham.

Making my way down Friar Lane.

Down to the Market Square.

Down to my town.

To my local.

# The Joseph Else

*Been shagging any more beasts lately?* Wilko roars on my arrival.

His fast eyes dart around the high table, looking for reinforcement, which he gets via a wave of grins and guffaws.

He expects me to shrink but I grow.

*Damn right, Wilk,* I announce, standing proud. *You should have seen this state last night, Li'l Ron. Makes Quaz look like Scarlett Johansson. Fucking obscene, pal.*

The noise is neutralised. Wilko doesn't know what to do with this. A piss-weak smile slits the centre of his pig face.

*Is that possible?* he counters, unsure.

This secret victory is more pleasurable than I ever imagined.

*Li'l Ron, mate, I don't know why I do it. Like you say, I'm not a bad-looking lad.*

These two lines act as a double-blow sucker punch. Showing audacity at the use of his first name and at the same time exposing a flicker of homosexuality. Maybe a third thread in being deemed *not a bad-looking lad*, which really means *a good-looking lad*, which Li'l Ron Wilk is clearly not.

Just like his daughter.

*This girl,* I say, *if you could call it that. Fucking hell. She must have been spawned by some proper ugly parents to end up like that.*

Wilk uncomfortable under the spotlight. His assault on full backfire.

The table goes edgy. Like, *who is this over-confident weirdo?*

He moves around, thinking of something else to say. At last, he manages, *Is it me or have you been wearing the same clothes for the last week? You chasing Shaun for the gold medal in the Tramp Olympics or what?*

The joke, without context to many of the new faces around the table, bombs.

*All right then*, Wilk concedes. *Go get yasen a drink then, kid.*

Things go back to normal. *At ease, gentlemen.* I turn my attention to Shaun of the Dead, who is maybe taking satisfaction in Wilk's failed attempt at humiliation.

*You got that score I lent you the other day, Shaun?*

He's taken aback by this new edge in my tone.

*Err, no, mate, I—*

I wave him off like I was half joking anyway.

The White Storm has lit my head and I don't really need another drink yet, but I buy one anyway and sit next to

## Turkish

We nod and sit silent for a while. Turk and I have a bond which we acknowledge but never talk about. What this bond is I couldn't conclusively define. Something different from the rest. Call it culture, call it class. Maybe cos we've heard of Albert Camus. Maybe cos we've travelled places other than Benidorm and Lanzarote. Maybe cos we use words with more than two syllables. Our kinship is one that the others wouldn't notice. I sense the same comfort in him that I feel. To be able to have *an actual conversation*.

Time passes. Our glasses empty.

*Would you care for another?* he says.

I feel what Shaun must feel in the face of charity. *Relief.* Nah, relief not strong enough. *Salvation.*

*You're out of money, aren't you?* he says with psychic wonder.

*How you know?*

*I've been watching you.*

*Eh?*

*Your demise over the last three days. It's quite frightening.*

*What are you talking about?*

*Have you seen yourself in the mirror?*

*What?*

I catch myself in the empty pint glass. Turkish's face is serious.

*You need to stop drinking*, he says gravely.

*Are you taking the fucking piss?*

*You need to stop.*

*We're in a pub.*

*Yes, we are.*

*Well, Turkish, here in England there's a phrase – pot calling kettle.*

*I know this phrase.*

I'm wondering when the brown boy is gonna shut the fuck up and get to the bar.

*But I am functioning*, he says at last.

*Meaning?*

Everything Turkish does is cool and slow. He sighs, moves his head, looks into his empty glass like it's a crystal ball.

*My guess is, you've probably taken out a good portion of your life in these days.*

Suddenly I am naked, scared to death. A bubble burst only for reality to come flooding in.

*I'll deal with that tomorrow*, I say.

*And the next day and the next day and the next day.*

Turkish is starting to get on my nerves. I look at Shaun on the next table and consider switching company.

*I'm functioning*, he repeats.

I look down and away and then back again. Then around at the rest of the people.

*Most of the people here are functioning*, Turkish adds. *Wilk is functioning.*

I look up at my fat foe, cracking another joke, belly laughing.

*Some of us hold down jobs. Stay out of hospital, and prison.*

*What about Shaun?* I say.

*He too is not functioning.*

I feel ashamed at being roped in with that tramp.

*Anyone else?* I say in a sour kind of tantrum.

Turkish goes around the room with his eyes.

*Your friend Fry.*

My friend Fry. My friend. Not anymore he isn't.

*You know he hasn't got long to live, right?*

*Fuck you talkin' about?*

*Have you seen his hands?*

*What about them?*

*Swollen, like balloons. A very bad sign. Means his liver is failing.*

*Fuck you know?*

This high-and-mighty prick was starting to get on my nerves.

*Oh, all this functioning/not functioning bullshit*, I say philosophically. *What's it matter anyway? The difference between a slow death and a fast one.*

*That's one way to put it.*

*What's another way to put it?*

*No you're right*, Turkish says, standing at last. *It all ends at some point.*

I expect a punchline. A final word. But one doesn't come and I'm left hanging, staring into my empty. Then my thoughts go to my poor friend. My poor Fry and how I fucked him over today. *Dead grandma and getting his emotions back.* I replay the scene through my head then something really dark grabs me. Remembering how he turned away from me in the street. How he took a right into Stannz and not straight on into town and back to his yard. Where was he going, what was he after? Now I'm crippled by a fear that I may have just pushed him into a relapse.

*It all ends at some point*, Turkish had said. *Hasn't got long ... his hands, his liver.*

All this is true, yet my nihilism is in doubt cos all I wanna do right now is go find him. Track him down. Save him. Save my friend.

As Turkish returns with the pints, an almighty cheer and laughter sounds off next to us, a deep drumming on the table.

### Li'l Ron Wilk & Shaun of the Dead

An act of sadomasochism between two heterosexual men. A small crowd gathers around Shaun, cheering.

He's walking around the pub like a chicken, half laughing, half something else. Wilk is pulling people in to look at him.

*Cluck, Shaun, cluck! Louder, Shaun, louder. Legs higher, you smelly cunt. I wanna see a chicken, a proper chicken.*

While he does this, Wilk flicks coins at him; twenties, fifties, the odd pound.

Shaun never takes his eyes off them, chasing them down as he goes. A gold coin rolls under the table. Shaun on all fours, dragging himself across the carpet.

*Enough chicken time, Shaun. Pig! We wanna see a pig.*

More people throw more coins.

Wilk starts running lines from the film *Deliverance*.

*Squeal like a pig, boy!*

Something gives way in Shaun. I watch it break in his face.

*No more, Wilk, please.*

Wilk now takes to his knees, pulling out his wallet, pulling out a crisp twenty-pound note. *Piss your pants, pig, and this is yours.*

Shaun's eyes widen, hope and humiliation switching faces and then back again.

*C'mon, pig, piss yasen and it's all yours.*

On his hands and knees, head upturned, greasy hair stuck to the side of his face.

*But ... I can't ... I won't ... I mean, I don't need one.*

Wilk pulls the purple note away.

*Okay*, Shaun squeals.

I watch the faces watching this. Some blank, some appalled, most just having the best night's entertainment in a long time.

Just then it appears. Shaun's jeans darken as the urine slowly spreads. Crowd goes wild. Next, it pisses through material and fills the carpet. People leap back, amazed. Turkish takes his drink and moves elsewhere. I go to follow him but I can't. I need to see this.

Part of me cries. Part of me laughs.

Wilk goes to put the money back in his wallet for the final nail in the coffin, but the crowd won't allow this. The mob wouldn't accept this injustice. Honour amongst thieves.

Shaun has earned his dollar. His crust. His wage.

For the first time, Wilk is bullied into paying Shaun his wages.

He now stands with it, arms aloft as the crowd cheers.

Drenched in piss. Stinking the room out with a new odour to add to the collection of his old ones.

I don't understand this.

Or maybe ... I understand it too much.


Either way, I need another drink.


### Wounding with Intent

It catches my eye on the way to the toilet. Dark wooden handle with a thick serrated blade. It hasn't been used. Nice and clean, spotless. For some reason, I pick the steak knife up and put it in my pocket without really thinking about it. While I piss, I wonder what this means. Why have I done this? When I rejoin the mob, my attention turns to Wilk. I watch him. I watch his physicality. I watch his movements. I think about him. Who he is and the way he treats people, belittles people, harms people. Even now, he is verbally tearing into some young punk who has no choice but to sit and take it, laugh it off. All in the name of pub banter, yet when the same playfulness is turned against him it becomes *disrespect* and warrants a wallop, a backhand across the face to *keep in line*, to *not take liberties.* The underworld was full of backward codes. Wearing the face of integrity when really all it did was keep the tyrannical hierarchy going. You could lie, cheat, beat, rob a house, shag someone's Mrs (providing they were a lower rank), but God forbid you should *grass*. Grassing was the ultimate dirty, not because of some deep moral fibre but simply because it kept people at the top of the food chain instead of being slammed up in the pen. No one seemed to question this conundrum. They do – like most people in all walks of life – accept rules without challenging them.

I carry on watching Wilk and something about him knows this. He starts taking furtive little glances through the back mirror. Maybe my kamikaze attitude earlier has put him on edge. Maybe he saw me take the steak knife, which now feels very alive in my pocket. For a few seconds, I wonder where my mind is at, where it has *gone*. To a dark, dark place. An invincible world of no consequences. I had the rep of being *a lover not a fighter* and this much is true. I acted hard sometimes as a way of getting out of bother. Acted hard but I wasn't. With my height, and a stoneface, I could sometimes pull off an air of menace but it was all a ruse. Most of the time, I went down like a sack of shit. It didn't take much. One love-tap on the chin and I was gone. I've probably been sparko'd about half a dozen times in my life, only I never seemed to learn. One day will be my last one. One day, I will gob off at the wrong man and my days will be done. It's only a matter of time. Law of averages and all that.

Today is a new feeling, though, cos I have a six-inch friend with me. Sharp against my skin and really I should be careful. Forget about it and sit down sudden and I could end up shivving myself. Imagine that in the papers. *Pisshead stabs himself to death with a Wetherspoons steak knife.*

Wilk is back on Shaun again. As if getting him to cluck like a chicken and squeal like a pig and then piss himself isn't enough, now he's on to something else. I look at Wilk and fantasise about sticking him one. I regard the size of him, his bulk no longer a weapon of intimidation but just more meat to carve up. My eyes never leave the width of his chest and the heart that beats inside it.

In the end, I pull out the knife and slam it down on the table. Grab Shaun by the scruff of the neck, dragging him out of the pub.

*Where we goin'?*

*To get a drink, where d'ya think.*

*You got money?*

Once outside, I let him have it.

*Where the fuck is your self-respect?*

*What you on about?*

*That fucking animal show in there.*

Shaun is genuinely confused. *What? It was just a laugh. I'm a laugh, aren't I? Everyone was laughing, wasn't they?*

*Yeah, at you, not with you.*

*Nooooo, it's all right. Wilk's all right.*

This look on Shaun's face. Like he doesn't see the deeper meaning.

*Shameless.*

I say more but he just laughs it off.

I need a line that will get through, words that will perforate this shameless shield.

At last I find it:

*When did you stop being a man?*

That worked.

His face freezes for a moment.

A realisation so sudden and so stark it stops him breathing.

*C'mon, Robin, give me a break, mate.*

The conversation has carried us across the Square and now we are directly outside Yates's.

I become really emotional all of a sudden. *You're dying, Shaun. You're fucking dead.*

Shaun's eyes, large, colourless and solemn. *What choice do I have?*

I feel my own eyes shrinking into small slits of hate. *What?*

*Can't we just go in THERE?* he says, nodding at the *next pub.*

A slap finds its way across Shaun's face.

I'm just as shocked as he is.

Then another slap and another one.

The act of slapping.

*Don't, Robin, please, STOP.*

I haven't lost control like this in years, and I'm not sure what is actually happening.

*Please*, yelps Shaun. *I can't TAKE it anymore.*

It's the word *take* that finally stops me. Something *bigger picture* about the way he says it, way he *stresses* it. It disturbs me. Snaps me out of it. Snaps me out of myself. He's crying and so am I.

Find myself hugging him and he's hugging me back. A desperate strength to the man I didn't know was there. The last thing left.

All the nasty smells of Shaun's destitution must have melted away.

I take his distraught face and look right into it.

Into the snot and tears and pain.

Into his history, his lostness.

*Next time he or anyone does that to you, Shaun, next time anyone tries to rob you of your soul, you take the nearest glass or bottle and you stick it in their neck, you hear?*

Still crying, still heartbroken.

*You hear?* I say, I shout.

*I will, I will. I swear to God I will.*

There is a clenching of the teeth that makes me believe him.

Eventually, he nods. Eventually, he gets it. Eventually, he *sees*.


### Yates's Wine Lodge

In Yates's and it's like nothing's happened. All the emotions and bonding and big life/bigger picture stuff is gone and it's exactly as we were. Back to business. Back to normal. *Why do I even bother?* Shaun has swooped and swiped a pair of pints and he's laughing his head off, proud of his art. It's this art that becomes the centre of conversation now. We stand upstairs, looking down. Not at the people. Not at the lads we might know or women we want to know. But we are looking at their drinks.

*You've got to do your homework*, Shaun of the Dead begins.

He talks like he's doing the commentary for a wildlife show, or lecturing at university.

This is his area of expertise.

*It's a gold mine out there*, he says, full of enchantment. *People are out, having a good time. Dancing. Pulling. Fucking about. They don't have time to be watching their drinks all night, and that's where I come in. Honestly, Robin, you watch me closely and you'll never have to pay for a drink again.*

Where my life is heading, this is a life skill I need to pick up.

Learning from the masters.

Raising from Fry.

Swiping from Shaun.

My future is bright.

## Coach & Horses

With our new brotherhood on board, I decide to let him in on a little secret.

*I fucked Wilk's daughter.*

He almost spits out his drink. *Fuck me.*

*Nope, fuck her. I did last night.*

*Kimberly?*

*Yep.*

*Thought she was a lettuce licker?*

*What can I say,* I wink, *she was back on the meat diet last night.*

His face lights up. His eyes shine. His shoulders bobbing up and down, dark laughter.

*I wondered what you were going on about earlier, in Wethers. Thought it was a bit weird.*

Shaun isn't as unaware as I first thought.

*Fuck me, Robin, don't ever let him find out.* He puts his hand out in between us. *I mean, NEVER let him find out.*

*I wasn't planning to.*

*Hey, don't worry, I won't say owt. You've been good to me, Robin. I know where my loyalty lies.*

*Shaun, it's cool. I wouldn't have said owt if I didn't think I could trust you.*


## Reflex

Eighties-theme club.

Bright colours, bold artwork:

*Top Gun.*

Wham!

Mr. T.

Bananarama.

Toilets – He-Man on the men's, She-Ra on the women's.

Disco balls and Rubik's cubes.

A revolving dance floor turns through it.

I watch Shaun stand in the centre. By the time he does a 360, he is equipped with two full fresh pints. He really is an artist. A Picasso of the swipe world.

It's wall-to-wall fanny in here, but I'm more entertained by watching Shaun's work.

Drinks from under noses. He swipes from the DJ, a bouncer.

A whole fish bowl from a hen do. Eight straws, four each. We down the whole lot in about a minute.

Songs from the period play through our night.

*And we don't have to take our clothes off, to have a good time, oh no ... I think we're alone now, there doesn't seem to be anyone around ... The only way is UP, baby, for you and me now ...*


## Upper Parliament Street

A great night and a new friendship. The company I keep. This is it now. A new life ahead of me, I've decided. I've decided to stop battling *all this* and just accept it. *Go surrender!* I've got everything I need right here on the streets. They are paved with gold. Fry has taught me that. Shaun of the Dead has taught me that. Time to give up and let it be. Jump off the wagon and stay off the wagon and let the good times roll.


## Tesco Express

Shaun and I bolt through the door. A fat but fast security man after us. A six-pack of Stella each. One of the cans splits from the rest and hits concrete. Somehow, Shaun steps on it and he's up in the air. Like a cartoon character. Landing on the flat of his back and the security man is on top of him. A small crowd cheer at the scene. I wait around a bit, watching as he is led back into the shop.

A night at the Hotel Bridewell for Shaun of the Dead.

A bed, and a roof over his head.


## Rock City

then Stealth. None of the cunts will let me in so I head home. Head somewhere. The Forest, the graveyard. I follow the curve of the shiny tramline, up alongside the Arboretum. I follow it until I reach a human leg. Casually draped over the cold iron. An ankle ready made, to be cut in two. Something frighteningly familiar to all this. A body lying face down on the floor. I grab it and drag it and turn it. A face looking up at me. I know this face. I know this eye. This unmistakable eye. This eye belonging to


### Boz

*Boz. What the fuck.*

Recognition sparks in *that* eye. The raw hatred almost giving him superpower, bringing him back to life. A deep furrow in the centre of his forehead. A spit bubble bursts over his lip.

He snorts. He snarls.

He tries to speak but it just won't come.

The bell of a tram chimes through the dark, passing us, running over the track where his ankle was just moments ago.

*Boz, man, chill.*

I have him on his feet, over my shoulder, around my neck. He's twice the size of when I last saw him. Packed on the pounds. His wrecked face glazed with greying stubble. Somehow, we work a soundless system of navigation. He points and I follow. We head back in town. Rounding off towards the Meadows, by the precinct, by the water's edge; dark floodlights etched into the night sky from both football grounds, separated by the Trent.

Through the whole mission, Boz can only manage the one word. A name he keeps saying over and over. *Heather, Heather, Heather.*

His pad is bad. She's obviously done one, long gone, and this is the aftermath: an alcoholic's squalor. Empty cans everywhere. Pizza boxes and slimy takeaway containers. I throw Boz on the sofa and for the first time I realise I don't know his name. His actual name. He's awake but still stupefied, incapable of words or free movement.

I pour him a pint of water and put it by his head.

Sitting staring at a framed photo I hadn't noticed. The thinnest crack running through the centre of her face. Heather. The picture does her too much justice in my view. She doesn't look like that in *real life.*

*I miss her, mate. I really fucking miss her.*

*I know you do. I know.*

I wanna say more but I can't think of more, of anything else other than:

*You know we're not anything, don't you? Heather and me. It was all in the past and it was fuck all even then.*

He doesn't say anything. He doesn't do anything.

*And you wanna see something else?* I say.

His good eye looks at me. The other stays on Heather's face.

*You wanna see this big dick I keep going on about?*

His forehead furrows again. A heavy breath and a return of that hatred. He tries to move but can't.

*This is what you're up against, brother. Here's the competition.*

I stand over him and undo my belt, unbutton, zip.

I pull it out and show it to him.

A serene smile moves across his face. A new handsomeness there. He lets out two soft chuckles. A peace in his eyes that I have not seen in a human before.

With that, he falls, falls into a deep untroubled sleep.


### Make Your Bed

Then I get a strange instinct to do something.

Clean. Tidy up.

I blitz the joint. Almost maniacally. Top to bottom and it sobers me right up.

Wash all the pots. Bin all the junk.

Even make his bed and run a Hoover over the carpet. Mop the bathroom and the kitchen. When I'm done, I find a pen and paper and leave a note by the kettle, near which I have placed a cup with a teabag in it, ready for when he wakes up in the morning.

The note, a quote from some book I once read:

*Well, it's a good life and a good world, all said and done, if you don't weaken.*

I leave and lock up and post the key.

Start walking the night. Walking the city like so many times before. Long through its bones and corridors. I walk forever. Walk until my feet are sore and my mouth is dry.

Then I remember something, and my heart skips a beat.

171

# Robin & Robin

White Storm in one of the arches. There's not much of it left. Nowhere near as much as I imagined. Just a slanted line of black liquid through the tilt in the bottle.

I take it and open it and sip it.

I turn and face the Robin Hood statue in the centre of the clearing, his bow and arrow pointed right at me. I stand on the slab of concrete and face him. His features flattened and eroded from all the years. All the weathers.

*Robin, man. What a night it's been. What a day. What a week.*

I jump off the slab and land on the flat of my feet, looking up at him.

*But you and I both know this has to end now. This,* I say, raising the bottle at him, *has to be my last drink, my last bottle. And not just tonight. But forever. Turkish was right. I have taken out life in four days. And if I carry on, I'll take out more. I'll take out all of it. I may even take out someone else's, if I haven't already. I can't drink. I've proved this time and time again. One drink means a dozen, and one night means a week. I've tried to regulate myself but it never works. Only drink on special occasions. Only drink at the weekends. Only drink after 7 o'clock, 5, 4, 3 2, 1. But the morning always finds me. So tomorrow I will stop. It won't be easy. It will be hard. It will be hell. Right now, I feel grand, great. Like you, Robin, I am a true outlaw and enjoy the chase. But tomorrow I shall be as weak as a kitten. Everything will scare me. But I have to push through that. Rattle through this. Remember this conversation and draw from your example. After, I will stay in bed for a long time. I will simply do nothing. Let the world take on my weight and work around me. I will eat, read, sleep. Drink loads of water. Drink loads of tea. Milk, soup. I will wait for summer. In time, I may get a job. In time, I may get a girl. But all will be gentle, all will be slow. I will have neat little systems for all things. I will look after my mind. Mind, this is the most precious gift and I will guard it with my life. I will guard my sobriety too. I will treat it like a project. I will treat it like a plant. I shall water it and give it light. Nurture it and watch it grow – day by day, year by year. Oh, I have a lot of shit to face first, I know that, Robin Hood, Prince of Thieves. People have been hurt. Crimes have been committed. It may take a while for people to trust me again. Drink explains my actions, but it doesn't excuse them. I will not shy away from the evil forces I have created through my misdeeds. I will meet them head-on. Put my hands up and take what's coming. I'll be all right, though, Robin, I know I will. I know I will because I'm a good person, see. Bit of a cunt at times but on the whole a good egg. I know I may not be making much sense right now but letting rip like this, well, I'd say it's something like an epiphany. A long farewell to the old life and the start of a new one. I'm hanging up my gloves, mate. Come tomorrow, I'm a brand spanking new human being. A good lad. A good lad. A really good fuckin' little lad.*

I leave the empty bottle on Robin's boot, chopping back through, and into the night.

### Sherwood Rise

Climb up the fire escape and knock on for what seems like an hour. At last, his face appears at the window, scrunched up with sleep, on the other side of the glass.

He opens up and lets me in.

*I'm so sorry about earlier*, I say.

Fry doesn't say anything, just gets back into bed, facing the wall.

*About earlier*, I repeat. *I'm so sorry.*

*What you on about?*

*Man at the off-licence ... which one bothers you most?*

*Which one bothers me the most, between what?*

*It's what I said.*

*Just go to sleep, Robin.*

The dark outline of him moves closer to the wall.

*Hey, Fry, you didn't relapse, did you?*

*What?*

*Didn't buy owt, did you?*

*No!*

*And your hands, they're all right, aren't they?*

*You're off your fuckin' head, bruv.*

I get the sleeping bag from the corner of the room and roll it out under the window.

*Tonight has been magic, man. Signs everywhere. All through these days, I've been given sign after sign after sign. Only now I am starting to learn the language.*

*What fuckin' language?*

*The language of the universe.*

*Fuck's sake.*

*You might be right about this God business, Fry. You might actually be right.*

I tell him more of the story since leaving him in the Square. Quaz, Boz, Darren, Kimberly and Luna. All the people from Wetherspoons and everything that's happened.

He says nothing.

He must have fallen asleep.

From there, I lay and listen to the blowing of the tree outside. That too finally stops as the sun comes up.

Day Five

# The Rat

'Well, it's a good life and a good world, all said and done, if you don't weaken.'

Alan Sillitoe, *Saturday Night and Sunday Morning*

# Irreversible

*Fry dies in my sleep and a rat scurries over my foot. I gasp and kick it off. White tide of turquoise water touches the golden beach of a deserted island to the music of Caribbean Blue. Breadcrumbs in the bed. Fry stands crooked in the doorway.* Off to get my methadone, *he says.* Methadooorrrnnnee so I can get my emmoorrrrtiooonnns *back. Footsteps. Voices under the floorboards. Slam of a door. I shudder, brother. This is it. Delirium tremens delusional terrors, tremors. I am walking down a red tunnel. When I get about halfway, it snaps in half. I watch the rest of it fall through space. Hear French voices. Police siren mixed with a child's laughter. Radio:* Life is a rollercoaster, just got to ride it. *Fry waves at me through his window with a giant hand.* Can't stay here, bruv, you'll get me thrown out ... and I'm already infested with rats. *Two more run over my leg and I gasp and kick out. Open my eyes. So much daylight. Not slept properly in days. Glass of water by my head. Robin Hood statue is talking to me, telling me things. Secrets. White Storm is on his boot. Gasps and kicks it off. A boy holding his mother's hand, walking backwards, by the castle. Caves rumble underneath. Earthquake. Boz sitting up on his sofa, spitting feathers, smiling. He gets up and goes to his sparkly clean kitchen to make a cup of tea. That silly mod haircut taped to the side of his face. Takes the tea; sipping it, slurping it. The picture of Heather is nowhere to be seen. A rat runs along a shiny tramline. Long whiskers, long tail. Stops at a leg hanging over the iron and starts to gnaw at it. I gasp and kick it away. Someone puts a penny in the jukebox. Jokebox.* We don't have to take our clothes off ... to have a good time, oh no. *Shaun of the Dead dressed as a cheerleader, doing cartwheels on the revolving dance floor. Swooping and swiping drinks. Kimberly catches him in the act and punches him full in the mouth. She starts beating the shit out of him. More girls join in. Cavegirl is there, clubbing him with an inflatable penis. At last, he is put in handcuffs and taken away. Turkish sits watching it all while reading his book,* Women in Love *by D.H. Lawrence. A rat runs over my naked stomach and I cry out. Bottles of White Storm under every arch and I'll never run out. I hand one of them to Jack Lemmon. Asian off-licence man getting ready to go to a funeral. Dressed in black. He stands over two graves. Side by side. One headstone reads 'Fry's Grandma', and the other reads 'Darren'. I move on to his shoulder and whisper gently in his ear,* Which one bothers you the most? *Next, laughter crashes in on me from everywhere and I feel like I'm about to wake up. Scarlett and Cheryl hush me back to sleep, hold my head and dab my eyes, feed me grapes. Wearing matching bikinis. A blue two-piece set with dolphins on. A big booming sound from the war cannons in the Arboretum makes me jump. Now they are wearing outfits from the 1950s. Scarlett as Marilyn Monroe, Cheryl as Sophia Loren. From nowhere, I am bundled into the back of a white van, taking me back to Carlton Hill. Wilk is driving, daughter in the passenger seat. Neither knows I am hiding in the back. Scared to death. Two rats run around my feet and I grit my teeth to save me from screaming. They can't know I'm here. Sneak out and find Cassidy in a phone box. It's Cassidy's physical form but my mother's soul. She is asking me what's wrong. She's asking me to come home. GILF then takes my hand and leads me back into the pub, The Free Man. She plops her large fake breast into a pint of cider and says,* SUCK. *Standhill Road. Things calm and get warm. No more rats. No more danger. Just a feeling of safety and goodness. Windchimes. Luna and I. We are giggling under a cloud-white, cloud-soft duvet. I pinch her nose and she laughs. Golden sun streams through our room, bathing everything in ethereal light. Her bare brown smooth soothing body underneath me. The sound of the shower, a waterfall. Water running over soft rocks. An eagle cuts across the perfect blue. Sobriety, she says. The future, she says. You found me and saved me for a reason. The summer is ours. Her kiss is so real, and Jeremy Kyle's voice comes from somewhere.* Well well well well. The lie detector results are back, those all-important DNA results. Robin Goode, you are the father of the child. *Football cheers of a Saturday afternoon crowd from the City Ground.* There's only one little Robin, one little Robin, there's only one little Robin. *Luna wears a wedding dress and is crying happy tears. We're getting married and Miguel plays his Spanish guitar. Her dad, Luigi, walks her down the aisle. When he sees me, he smiles and says,* I forgive you for smashing my windows, motherfucker, hahaha. *Everybody laughs and the ceremony starts.* Do you take this woman to be your lawfully wedded wife? ... I do. *Cassidy catches the bouquet. At the reception, Luna and I slow dance to our wedding song,* Move Over Darling. *The mood suddenly darkens as another song gate-crashes it halfway through.* Dooms Night. Whhhaaauuummm. Whhhaaauuummm. Whhhaaauuummm. *Luna screams and points at the dance floor.*

*Where Darren stands in the centre of it, Adidas trackies around his ankles. Rubbing his two-inch veiny knob with one hand and doing his DJ dance with the other. The whole room freaks out. A demented Darren, blocked-up Hoover voice,* Oh, pucking sit on my pucking face, ya pucking bitch! *Next, I am being chased through the streets by everyone – Boz; Kimberly; Luna's dad; dads of the underage girls; cavegirls trying to club me; Marianne; Wilk and Vic. I am chased into the city centre, through the market square. The only person not after me is Whycliffe, who keeps shouting out,* Can I sing you a song? *Mario Brothers music plays over the sequence. Crazy computer sounds; beeps and bleeps and buzzes as I collect mushrooms and disappear down green pipes. The police then join in on the chaos.* Stop or we'll set the rats on you! *Suddenly I hear awful rodent sounds followed by small bites on the backs of my ankles. I gasp and kick them off. I try to wake up but can't. A real raw hellish feeling grips my being ... horrors, night terrors, sleep paralysis.*

*Next, there is calm, and a dark wind rolling over my face. Three figures sit me down. Quaz, Boss and Brian Clough ... they take it in turns to talk ... Quaz:* My name is actually Rox and you should start calling me that from now on ... you're a good man, Robin, but you've got a lot to learn, a lot to let go of ... *Boss coughs into her fist:* You're a lucky bastard too. Lucky I covered for you ... lucky I got you out the shit ... you're lucky Darren's cut wasn't that bad ... lucky no one else found out. I managed to sweep it under the carpet; otherwise, we'd both be doing prison sentences ...I can't have you back, though ... that's obvious, right? But overall you're a very lucky man. *Brian Clough stands up and adjusts his green jumper, walks slowly up towards the lighted neon of the Hard Rock Cafe ...* Now then, lad, *he says,* now then, son ... now then, young man, they're putting a statue of me up there in November ... suppose you'll be talking to me too ... only it's not really me, just a representation of me ... why do you do that, talk to statues? You do know that there's nobody there ... that you're just talking to yourself ... or are you? Cos sometimes you get something back, don't you? Like THIS, like NOW. These voices from the other side, from the inside ... and that there, my dear son, is the answer to the God Question. The answer you've been trying to find out for the past—

I wake up with a sudden gasp. Like emerging from from an icy lake.

There's a siren somewhere and the TV is on.

A weather report.

## Lucy Kite

I get up and turn her off. Her image is replaced by black. Almost like those old-fashioned TVs. A tiny dot of disappearing white. I gaze into the screen at the dark reflection of the room. Outside, and I can't tell the time. A murky grey, which could mean that the day was either fading or just beginning. I could have slept right the way through. That is a distinct possibility. I don't know how long I've been knocked out. Feel like I have slept through something big. Fry is face down, his body to the wall, half wrapped in a duvet. A near-full bottle of White Storm is beside him.

I find my missing sock and put it back on. Followed by my shoes.

I go over and pull the duvet over his bare shoulder.

I look out of the window one last time. The tree is still.

## Goodbye, Fry

Walking the length of 4th Avenue, back onto the Rise. Pop in the garage to buy a bottle of water and surprised to see a scrunched-up fiver in the corner of my wallet. Shaun would call this *admission fee*. Just enough dollar to get you a seat at the table. I head through the Forest and down Mansfield Road. Passing boozers but none of them tempt me. Lincolnshire Poacher. Golden Fleece. Even The Peacock with its reparative properties. In the distance, I see a tall, good figure and think of Marianne. It's her, I'm sure, but I'm probably wrong.

## The Joseph Else

Only it's not The Joseph Else because a figure stops me at the door, stops me from going inside.

# Vic

*I wouldn't fucking go in there if I was you.*

His eyes glaze over like marbles.

*What?*

*You.*

*What about me?*

*Fucking do one if I was you.*

*Vic?*

*Fucking trouble you've caused.*

He looks over his shoulder once and then twice.

Then over my shoulder too.

The suspense is killing me and I'm back with that need again. A need to drink more than ever.

*You gonna fuckin' tell me then or what?*

No one ever spoke to Vic like this, but desperation had other plans. Whatever it was must be bad cos my attitude seems to bypass him.

*I'd walk away while you've still got legs.*

I look inside the pub to an eerie funeral atmosphere. The calm *after* the storm.

Again, he looks over his shoulder. Then:

*Shaun come in first thing this morning, opening time. He comes in straight from a night in the holding cells. Reckons you got him arrested after bullying him into nicking a crate of Nelson.*

*What?*

*Then he told Wilk that you've been knobbing his daughter.*

My blood runs cold.

Shaun.

The rat.

*We couldn't believe our fuckin' ears. Just comes right out and sez it. In front of every cunt. I dunno, in his deluded way, he must have thought he was doing a good deed. Loyalty or whatever else was going on in his fucked-up head. Scoring brownie points. Probably thought Wilk was gonna hug him and put fifty quid in his rocket. Well ... you can imagine the fucking embarrassment, the shame of a thing like that. One of the lads slipping his baby girl a length. In front of a pub full of people. So Wilk obviously had to give him one. His trademark backhand, knocks Shaun right off his stool. And that's when it happened.*

These words are passing me like a dream, like *the* dream.

Vic coughs into his fist, clearing his throat for the grand finale.

*Shaun does no more than smash the nearest pint glass and shove it in Wilk's neck.*

Now I'm expecting Vic to break character. Something in his face to change and give him away, showing me that this was a joke, a wind-up.

It never does.

*Think he's killed the cunt.*

I step back and stare at Vic, the burst vessels on his purple nose.

*Size of the gash and how far it went in. Matter of hours, mate. Wilk's dead.*

I stare into more space.

*And Shaun?* I say, at last.

*Done one. Half the city looking for him. I hope the pigs catch him before they do. You're just lucky that all the attention is on him and not you.*

*What the fuck have I got to do with it?*

*You kind of started the ball rolling on this one, Robin.*

*That's fuckin' bollocks.*

*Look,* Vic puts something in my hand, a wad of notes, *get yasen out of the city for a few days. Let it blow over and, in the meantime, I'll see what I can do.*

*See what you can do?*

*I'll have a word. I'll sort it.*

I feel eyes everywhere. A grip around my neck.

*Go,* says Vic.

I do. I go. I'm gone.


## Friar Lane & Beyond

Nearest off-licence. I find it and a bottle finds me. All thoughts of giving up and the new life and sobriety get put on hold, not even a consideration now. The hurt for thirst is as intense as it ever was. I step out and into a side street, heading down to the train station. Turning the lid of the White Storm but something is wrong. Something *isn't happening.* It isn't turning. The lid is stuck, jammed, cross-threaded. This is insane. I twist and twist, so much that the bottle starts to change shape. My fingers burn; red lines streak across the soft palms of my hand.

*Why won't this thing fuckin' open?*

I'm so dizzy and disoriented that I seem to be lost in my own city.

I look up to see a familiar landmark.

Medieval font stamped upon the white walls of Ye Olde Trip to Jerusalem: '1189AD. The OLDEST Inn in ENGLAND'.

I head down to the canals, walking the water's edge.

Nearing the train station, but where the fuck would I go?

Where would I run to?

Still, I keep on with the bottle, turning and twisting but nothing.

Then a feeling to slow it.

To stop it.

To slow and stop and sit down for a bit.

### Starbucks

Bentinck Hotel. The faded sign hangs over the canal, letters breaking out in the water's reflection. Up over the bridge, two men in suits are talking, pointing up at the old building, writing things down. One of them wears a green tie with a logo. Some sort of female mythological figure, white hair flowing under a crown.

*So how long are we talking then*? one of them says.

*A month, six weeks tops.*

*Smashing*, he says.

I watch the men disappear back into the building.

I stand slowly, leaving the bottle by the bench. Make my way up onto the bridge, back onto street level.

### 'God is a Comedian Playing to an Audience that is Too Afraid to Laugh.'

*Yo, is dat ting full?*

I look over the bridge at the bench where I was sat.

Two figures approaching.

One short, one large. Short leads, large trails.

Short looks around suspiciously before making a grab at the bottle.

*Man, dis ting is full ... now dat's what I'm talkin' about.*

*Sparky, man, you a fuckin' tramp.*
*Says you, man. Ya haven't brushed ya teet in weeks.*
*Least I've got teef ta brush.*
Sparky's bony white hand wraps the bottle.
*Fuck, man, what's up wiv dis shit?*
He moves his body around and tries it from another angle.
*What's up, ya scrawny cunt, not had your Weetabix? Give it here.*
Sidekick tries to take it off him but Sparky shrugs him off.
The smaller man puts it between his feet, pulling, twisting.
Hands shaking at the pressure.
*Give it here, ya pussy.*
Again, Sparky pushes his mate away.
Sparky, losing it now, tries to put it on his back teeth.
*Fuck you trying that for? You've got no teef.*
Twisting the bottle in his large loose mouth.
*Just leave it, man. Let's go pub.*
*Ya mad! It's a full bottle, bredrin.*
A woman walking by watches as a red-faced Sparky won't give
up.
At last, he does. *Go on then, Frankenstein!* Hands it to Sidekick.
He takes it and tries it, twists it again and again.
Sparky now laughing his head off. *Told ya, bredders, this is some
sick prank, yo! Bet there's some fiend out there filmin' dis shit.*
He looks around the canal, up towards me, so I duck behind the
bridge.
Sparky takes it back off him and tries again. Back to Sidekick,
who eventually loses his temper and dashes it on the ground and it
bounces into a bush. Sparky tracks it and chases it down, picks it up
and launches it at a wall. Both grown men are now fully assaulting
the plastic bottle. They jump up and down on it. Sparky slips on the
grass and Sidekick nearly falls in the water.
*This is sick, man.*
*Fuck this.*
They are raging and laughing at the same time.
*Just leave it, Spark.*
*Fuck dat, not now. We've come too far.*
Tries biting it again.
Then Sidekick does. *Fuck … fink I've just chipped my toof.*
*Hahahahahaha.*
*Bastard.*

Sidekick stands in the middle of the path, looking nonplussed as he tongues the chip in his tooth. People have to walk around him to get by. Sparky is now beside himself, throwing the bottle against anything he can find; the wall, the floor, a bin. Busting it on the side of a bench.

*Fuck dis shit.*

A blade comes out of his pocket, shining in the April sun.

A father with two daughters panics, turns, goes back the other way.

Sparky digs at the lid with his knife, over and over until he catches himself. *FUCK! Muthafuckin' bitch!*

Sidekick's face lights up on seeing this, standing dumb and upright, pointing at Sparky, whose hand, then arm, gets streaked in blood.

*Hahahahahaha, look at you, ya daft cunt.*

*Fuckin raasclaat ting, man.*

Sparky finally gives up, takes it with his good arm and hurls it through the air.

It goes high. Through the sky like a missile. Heading in my direction, light passing through it.

The whole city seems to spin in its dizzy reflection.


### Running

I get back to my flat. Freaked out by the pin-drop silence. The stillness is total. I stand in the doorway for ages, getting used to it all again. The familiarity is comforting, yet it's gonna take a while to build trust again. Each dark object seems to consider me. Nothing has changed, yet everything has changed. *I* have changed. Or is that just what I'm telling myself?

If not changed, then maybe just *a little different.* Yeah, we'll go with that for now. I look in the mirror at the five-day growth on my face. A small shabby beard. I get out of this five-day jumpsuit and jump in the shower. I go to town on my personal hygiene. I brush my teeth for at least five minutes straight, until I have a mouthful of minty blood.

The clothes I put in a bin bag and consider throwing them out for good, maybe even burning them in a bucket.

I towel off and put fresh clothes on.

I wear all white. Nike bottoms and a Fleetwood Mac *Rumours* t-shirt. The normal thing for me to do would be crash but for some reason I stay on my feet. Potter about. Somewhere in that I take the Scarlett Johansson picture down. Can't bear her eyes on me anymore. Then I take a glass of water and go stand at my back window, overlooking the school I went to so many moons ago. It's different now. One of those Americanized-style academies. The school field is exactly the same, though. That God-awful running track they made us run around in PE. White lines painted on the green grass.

There's a lad running around it right now even though it's a Sunday.

He goes round and round.

I drink the water, go for a piss, fill up the glass again and he's still at it.

I count five laps, ten, fifteen.

*Why the fuck is he doing this?* I think. *Going around in circles. Hasn't he got anything better to do?*

At last, he leaves the track and cuts across the car park.

I go to the front of my flat and watch him through that window.

He runs up the nose-breaking incline of Perlethorpe Avenue.

I watch him until he becomes a stick figure, a tiny dot on the brow of the hill.

I watch him until he disappears.